ROBIN
JONES
GUNN

I Promise

CHRISTY AND TODD
THE COLLEGE YEARS

BETHANYHOUSE
MINNEAPOLIS, MINNESOTA

Published by Bethany House Publishers
A Ministry of Bethany Fellowship International
11400 Hampshire Avenue South
Bloomington, Minnesota 55438
www.bethanyhouse.com

Printed in the United States of America by
Bethany Press International, Bloomington, Minnesota 55438

Library of Congress Cataloging-in-Publication Data

Gunn, Robin Jones, 1955-
    I promise / by Robin Jones Gunn.
        p.   cm. — (Christy and Todd ; 3)
    Summary: Christy believes her engagement to Todd to be a
dream come true, but instead they encounter turmoil and
conflict.
    ISBN 0-7642-2274-0
    [1. Weddings—Fiction. 2. Christian life—Fiction.] I. Title.
PZ7.G972 Ip   2001
[Fic]—dc21   2001001321

I Promise

From Robin Jones Gunn

THE CHRISTY MILLER SERIES

1 • *Summer Promise*
2 • *A Whisper and a Wish*
3 • *Yours Forever*
4 • *Surprise Endings*
5 • *Island Dreamer*
6 • *A Heart Full of Hope*
7 • *True Friends*
8 • *Starry Night*
9 • *Seventeen Wishes*
10 • *A Time to Cherish*
11 • *Sweet Dreams*
12 • *A Promise Is Forever*

Departures (with Wendy Lee Nentwig)
From the Secret Place in My Heart: Christy Miller's Diary

CHRISTY & TODD: THE COLLEGE YEARS

1 • *Until Tomorrow*
2 • *As You Wish*
3 • *I Promise*

THE SIERRA JENSEN SERIES

1 • *Only You, Sierra*
2 • *In Your Dreams*
3 • *Don't You Wish*
4 • *Close Your Eyes*
5 • *Without A Doubt*
6 • *With This Ring*
7 • *Open Your Heart*
8 • *Time Will Tell*
9 • *Now Picture This*
10 • *Hold On Tight*
11 • *Closer Than Ever*
12 • *Take My Hand*

THE GLENBROOKE SERIES

1 • *Secrets*
2 • *Whispers*
3 • *Echoes*
4 • *Sunsets*
5 • *Clouds*
6 • *Waterfalls*
7 • *Woodlands*

Mothering by Heart
Tea at Glenbrooke

01C

ROBIN JONES GUNN loves to tell stories. Evidence of this appeared early when her first-grade teacher wrote in Robin's report card, "Robin has not yet grasped her basic math skills, but she has kept the entire class captivated at rug time with her entertaining stories."

When Robin's first series of books for toddlers was published in 1984, she never dreamed she'd go on to write novels. However, one project led to another and *I Promise* is Robin's fifty-first published book. Other series include THE CHRISTY MILLER SERIES, THE SIERRA JENSEN SERIES, and THE GLENBROOKE SERIES. Combined sales of her books are over 2.5 million, with worldwide distribution. Many of the titles have been translated into other languages.

Robin and her husband, Ross, have been involved in youth work for over twenty-five years. They have lived in many places, including California and Hawaii. Currently they live near Portland, Oregon, with their teenage son and daughter and their golden retriever, Hula.

Visit Robin's Web site at *www.robingunn.com*

For all the Christys I have known.

May your promises last forever.

CHRISTY AND TODD · THE COLLEGE YEARS

1 Christy opened her eyes and focused on the empty bed across from her in the dimly lit dorm room. The digital alarm clock read 5:05 A.M.

Katie never came to our room all night. Where is she?

Getting up and snapping on the overhead light, Christy checked to see if Katie had left a note while Christy slept. No note.

Suddenly Christy stopped. Her fuzzy morning brain woke up. She remembered where she had been the night before and what had happened.

The Dove's Nest Café. We were all together. The whole gang.

A smile drew her lips heavenward as it all came back.

It wasn't a dream. Last night Todd asked me to marry him. And I said yes.

Opening the shades, Christy gazed outside. The streetlights that lined the campus of Rancho Corona cast a cool, bluish gray tint on the world outside her window. Rows of tall palm trees stood in a sacred hush waiting for the familiar breath of wind from the nearby desert to awaken them. Whenever the wind came, the palm trees danced, and something inside Christy compelled her to join them.

This morning she didn't need the rustling palm trees to call her heart to the dance floor. Inside, she already was twirling and spinning.

Todd and I are going to get married!

The phone rang, and Christy jumped to answer it.

"Hey, how's it going?" The deep voice on the other end was the same voice that had echoed in her sweet dreams all night.

"Hey yourself," Christy answered softly. "I was just thinking of you."

"Couldn't sleep?"

"I did a little. I woke up about ten minutes ago. Todd, did last night really happen? Did you really propose to me?"

"Yes, I did. And you said yes."

"Yes, I did."

"Yes, you did."

Christy closed her eyes and felt his voice's warmth wash over her.

"I spent the whole night playing my guitar," Todd said. "I'm working on a new song."

"How did your roommate feel about that? Or did you spend the night in the lobby?"

"I'm the only guy left in my wing. Everyone else

has gone home for Christmas break."

Christy remembered her missing roommate and asked, "Did you hear Katie say anything last night about going home?"

"No."

"I thought she was staying here this weekend with me, but she never came back last night."

"Did she stay in Sierra's room?" Todd asked. "She's done that in the past, hasn't she?"

"Yes. That's probably what she did. I know I shouldn't worry about her. She's a big girl and can take care of herself. It's just that with Katie I never know what's going to happen next."

"So, what are you doing right now?" Todd asked. "Do you want to meet me down by the chapel? We can watch the sunrise."

Christy laughed at the spark of spontaneity in his voice. "Sure, I'll be there in ten minutes."

Dressing in several layers in case it was as chilly outside as it looked, Christy paused only a minute in front of the mirror. Her long, straight, nutmeg brown hair was pulled back in a clip. She let it down and shook her head before giving her tresses a quick brushing. Todd liked her hair long. She smiled. Even though she had slept only four and a half hours, her blue-green eyes were bright and full of glimmering hope. Her cheeks had a rosy glow, and the longer she gazed at herself, the wider her smile grew.

So this is what a woman in love looks like. An engaged woman in love. A bride to be.

With a quick stop in the bathroom to wash her face and brush her teeth, Christy headed across the Rancho Corona campus to the small chapel at the mesa's edge. From the trail that ran along the rim of the school's property, the Pacific Ocean was visible on exceptionally clear days.

This morning a fine winter mist hovered low to the ground as Christy crossed the meadow. When the sun rose, it would be too hazy to see much of the view that stretched between the campus and the coast. She didn't mind. She wasn't trotting at such a fast clip to see the valley. She was going to meet her beloved, and she couldn't stop smiling.

Finding the door of the chapel open, Christy stepped into the sheltered warmth of the small, hushed building and spotted Todd. He was kneeling at the altar, eyes closed, head bowed.

With her heart still racing, Christy tiptoed to the altar. She knelt beside Todd. His short, sandy blond hair was wet. From him rose the subtle scent of Lifebuoy soap. As he lifted his head, his screaming, silver-blue eyes turned toward her. Christy immediately knew she wasn't the only one who had been smiling all night. The dimple on his right cheek seemed as if it had turned into a permanent mark.

Neither of them spoke. Their eyes did all the talking. Neither words nor touch were needed as they knelt there, silent before God and each other, talking to God, talking to each other. Heart to heart. Soul to soul.

Todd was the first to speak. It was a prayer of thanks. He asked God to direct their future steps and guide them as they made plans for their wedding. When he concluded, Christy joined him in saying "As you wish," which to them meant "Amen" or "May it be according to your will."

Todd stood and offered Christy his hand. "How does some breakfast sound?"

Christy smiled at how quickly Todd could go from intensely spiritual to immensely hungry. "Sure, I have the whole day free."

"Me too."

Hand in hand they stepped into the cool morning. The light from the sun broke through the mist like thin streamers made of silver glitter. The meadow before them had become a fairytale world, lit by tiny drops of light.

"It's so beautiful," Christy whispered.

"Let's get married right here," Todd said, stepping into the enchanted meadow.

Christy chuckled. "Okay. Right now?"

"I'm serious," Todd said. "Let's have the ceremony right here." He let go of her hand and, with wide arm motions, described the scene as he saw it. "We'll put an arch right here. Is that what you call those things you stand under? They're rounded on top and covered with flowers."

Christy nodded. "Yes, that would be an arch. Or a trellis."

"Let's get married right here under an arch." Todd

seemed to size up the field. "What do you think? We could fit enough chairs in here. You could wait over there in the chapel. When the music starts, you would walk down the aisle to here."

Todd stepped over to a spot where he stood in a direct line with the chapel. "This is where we'll put the arch. You'll come walking down the center there, wearing a white dress with some flowers in your hair, and I'll be waiting for you right here."

Christy's heart soared. "Sounds beautiful." She had assumed they would be married inside a church, but this meadow was as much a holy ground as a church, she thought. Especially this morning. Especially this very moment, with Todd's eyes lit up and the meadow sprinkled with a shimmering mist of celestial light.

"This would be a beautiful spot for an evening wedding," Christy said. "It would be too hot to sit out here in the afternoon in the summer."

Todd stopped. He turned to Christy. "Summer?"

"Don't you think it would be too hot to sit outside in the afternoon without any shade? I think August evenings are beautiful."

"August?" Todd repeated. "Are you thinking we should get married next summer?"

"Of course. We both will have graduated by then and had time to plan everything and—"

"I want to get married sooner than that," Todd said.

"Sooner? How much sooner?"

"I don't know. Next week is Christmas. Then we have the missions trip to Mexico with the youth group the week after that. What about the second weekend in January?"

Christy laughed. Todd didn't.

"Todd, we can't get married in three weeks!"

"Why not?"

"We have to plan everything! We have to find a place to live and buy rings and order invitations. I have to find a dress and—"

"You're great at planning things, Chris. That's what you do best. We have all of Christmas break to work on it."

"No, we don't. We're going to Mexico after Christmas, remember? We haven't even finished planning that trip yet."

"Okay, then how about the third week of January? Or the last week, right after I graduate?"

Christy felt panic rising inside. "Todd, how could we possibly pull off a wedding in a month? People will think we *have* to get married."

Todd's voice was calm and soothing as he reached for her hand. "You and I and everyone else know that isn't the case. Is that what you're afraid of? What other people think?"

Christy grasped Todd's hand tighter and tried to calm her rising emotions. "No, I'm not worried about what other people think. It's just that I would like our wedding to be special and well thought out. I want us to have enough time to plan everything the right way and not to feel rushed down the aisle. Does that make sense?"

Todd bent over and kissed Christy tenderly on the cheek. "Yes. That makes sense. What you're trying to tell me is that January is too soon."

"Yes, January is too soon." Christy wrapped her arms around him and rested her head on his shoulder. Her breathing returned to normal. She liked the idea of getting married here in the meadow. She could picture the two of them standing right here in the cool of the evening sometime next August.

Todd pulled away so he could look her in the face. "So, if January is too soon, what are you thinking? February?"

"No, I'm still thinking August would be best."

"August!" Todd laughed. "We don't need eight months to plan a wedding."

"Yes, we do."

"March." Todd held her at arm's length. "Easter vacation. It'll be perfect weather. You'll almost be done with school."

"Easter vacation is in April."

"Okay, then April. Not August. April. I want to marry you, Christy. I want to be with you. I want us to start our life together. This is what we've been waiting for."

"We've both been waiting, Todd. We've both been thinking and praying about it for almost six years. Eight more months is nothing. We can wait until August."

Todd looked out over the meadow. The risen sun now cast its filtered light through the mist, shining on the droplets of moisture that clung to the grass, turning them into tiny diamonds. All across the meadow it appeared as if the stars had fallen from the heavens and were scattered at their feet, creating new constellations in miniature.

Christy watched as Todd stuck out his chin and seemed to be processing all this with a firm determination. He was usually Mr. Whatever, laid back about everything. He had told her several months ago that he was inexperienced with things like birthday parties and holidays. Evidently he knew even less about planning weddings.

"Trust me, Todd," Christy said softly. "April is too soon."

"Yeah? Well, August is definitely too far away. We can fit in a wedding before this summer. I'm sure we can."

"Why fit it in? Why not wait until I graduate and have the wedding in June?" Christy asked. "The meadow will be beautiful in June."

Todd shook his head. "No, not June. It's looking like my position at the church will turn into full time on June first. I don't see how I could take a week off in June for our honeymoon."

"Maybe if you asked them now and explained—"

Todd turned his perplexed face toward Christy. "You know what? I don't want to talk about this right now. Let's get something to eat." He reached for her hand and started for the parking lot.

Christy noticed how the sun had pierced the morning clouds that previously had spread across the meadow. The glittering field of diamonds had evaporated, leaving a long stretch of dried winter grass. Nothing was enchanting about the world around them anymore.

Is this what happens when a match made in heaven tries to walk on the earth? How can the glimmering magic disappear so quickly?

Todd remained deep in his own thoughts as they drove into town in their Volvo station wagon. Christy told herself she should have been more spontaneous as they dreamed aloud about their wedding date.

I could have simply said yes to January or any other month. As soon as Todd was presented with the details, he would have changed his mind and adjusted to a more practical date. This is the time for me to be dreamy, not practical.

"It looks like that restaurant is open." Christy pointed to a café they were approaching. She hoped they could sit down and calmly discuss their wedding plans over a leisurely breakfast. This time around she would be less practical and more dreamy.

"I was thinking of a breakfast burrito," Todd said. "Do you mind if we go to Roland's Drive Thru?"

"I don't think there's a Roland's around here."

"I know one is near Doug and Tracy's house at the beach."

"That's a long drive. Are you sure you want to wait that long to eat?"

"I don't mind," Todd said. "Do you?"

Stop being so practical about everything! Just agree for once.

"Okay, Roland's is fine with me." *Even though it seems crazy to drive such a long way just to get a certain type of fast food.*

"Can we work on the Mexico trip?" Todd asked.

"What do you mean?"

"Can we start planning while we drive to Carlsbad?"

"You don't want to talk about our wedding date anymore?"

"Not now. I think a note pad is on the backseat. A pen should be in the glove compartment. It would help me a lot if we could work on the Mexico trip. Could you make a list like we did for the camping trip to the desert?"

Christy found the note pad and pen. In fat letters she wrote *MEXICO* at the top of the paper.

"We need tents," Todd said. "Could you put that on the list? And we need extra tarps, in case it rains."

As Todd continued with the list of what they needed, Christy took notes. All her letters came out thick and angry.

Why is it you can be practical about Mexico, Todd, but not practical about setting a wedding date?

The longer they talked, the longer the list became. Todd expressed surprise every time Christy thought of another necessary component of the trip, such as medical release forms for each teenager and whatever parental permission they needed to take the students across the border.

She wanted to say, "See? Every event takes careful planning. Especially something as huge as a wedding."

But she didn't. The frustration expressed itself only in the thick black printing that filled two pages on the note pad.

As soon as they exited the freeway in the beach town of Carlsbad, Todd rolled down his window. He seemed to need to fill his lungs with salty ocean air. Christy was glad for the fresh air, too. Her emotions had begun to spiral into a nose dive.

Where are all the lovey-dovey feelings I felt for Todd this morning? Why can't we spend the day dreaming about us? Did I ruin everything by not being spontaneous enough when he was in a dreamy mood?

"Hey, how's it going?" Todd said to the speaker box at the drive-through. "I'd like four breakfast burritos and two large orange juices." He turned to Christy. "What would you like?"

Christy tried to see the menu printed on the box outside Todd's window, but his arm blocked the sign. "Do they have French toast?"

"French toast?" Todd repeated as if he had never heard of such an item before.

"Never mind. I'll just have an egg and cheese breakfast sandwich and a milk."

Todd repeated her order and drove up to the window.

"Are you okay?" Todd asked.

Christy tucked her hair behind her ears and glanced at his handsome face. *How can I explain to you all the intense feelings colliding inside me for the past hour? I'm afraid that if I say anything, I'll be sorry later and hammer myself to pieces for making a big deal out of nothing.*

"I'm okay," Christy said in a low voice.

Todd paid the employee at the open window and handed the food to Christy. She was going to ask if he wanted to park the car so they could eat, but he turned left onto the main road, and she knew where he was headed. The call of the wild that always beckoned to Todd was the ocean. They were less than a mile from where the blue Pacific ran to meet the California coast. Christy knew she should have guessed that was why they had driven all this way for breakfast burritos. Todd wanted to eat their first breakfast as an engaged couple on the beach.

Only Todd didn't head for the beach. He turned toward the freeway.

"Are we going back to school?" Christy asked.

"No, I just thought we could share our breakfast."

Share our breakfast? What's he talking about?

Todd pulled the car to the side of the road under the freeway overpass and grabbed one of the large orange juices.

"Can you hand me two of those burritos?" he asked Christy. Then, leaving the engine running, Todd jumped out of the car and took the food to a homeless man huddled under a cardboard box. She hadn't noticed the guy when they had exited the freeway, but obviously Todd had.

As Christy watched Todd smile and offer the hot food to the surprised man, her heart beat a little faster. A troubling thought settled on her like an ominous shadow. *I'm going to spend the rest of my life with a man who is given to random acts of impulsiveness. I'm never going to know where we're going or what we're doing or with whom we'll be sharing our meals. Nothing will be predictable about our life together. Nothing orderly or steady or sure.*

Christy swallowed hard. Todd was jogging back to the car wearing a wide grin of contentment. She tried hard to press a welcoming smile across her face to greet him, but in her heart, all she could think was, *I don't know if I'm ready for this.*

2 Todd turned the car around and drove to the beach, where they parked and carried their breakfast over to a large, smooth boulder. Christy ate slowly, her eyes fixed on the endless ocean stretched out before them. She could feel Todd's gaze on her. Because they had sat together many times at the ocean without exchanging words, the silence felt familiar and had a comforting effect on her. Folding up the uneaten half of her breakfast sandwich, she let out a deep breath.

"Does it scare you?" Todd reached over to brush his fingers across Christy's cheek.

"Does what scare me?"

"Getting married. Or more specifically, marrying me?"

Unnerved at how Todd could read her thoughts, Christy threw up a smoke screen. "Why do you think I'm afraid?"

Todd traced the rim of her ear with his finger and didn't answer. She knew he was waiting for her.

"We don't think the same way," Christy blurted out.

"No, we don't."

Christy leaned her cold cheek against his warm hand. She decided to go ahead and hook a few of her fishy feelings onto the end of the line he patiently was holding over the deep waters of her heart. "Todd, I'm afraid that being married is going to be hard."

"Mmm-hmm."

"It will be a gigantic adjustment for both of us. We're opposites in so many ways."

"Mmm-hmm."

"You approach life differently than I do. You see things differently. I don't think the way you do."

"That's okay." Todd stroked her hair. "I don't see our differences as a problem."

"Of course you don't! That's my point. What's major to me is minor to you."

"I think our differences are good," Todd said. "We balance each other out."

"I think our differences will make it harder for us."

Todd lifted a handful of her long hair and brushed the ends across his lips.

"Todd, I don't think you and I know each other as well as we think we do. We have a lot of adjustments ahead of us."

"And a whole lifetime to work on them." Todd pulled her toward him so her head rested on his shoulder. In a calm voice he said, "Learning about each other and working through the adjustments are part of what makes a relationship alive and growing. I'm looking forward to that part of our future."

"I'm not," Christy heard herself say. "I think we're going to drive each other crazy. I'm so determined to have everything organized, and you're so spontaneous and so, so . . . random!"

"Yeah, I guess I am. What was it Katie called me a couple of months ago on our camping trip?"

"You mean when you brought plastic hangers instead of metal ones because you didn't realize I wanted to use them to roast marshmallows?"

Todd nodded.

"Katie said you were 'detail impaired.' "

Todd laughed. "That's right. And Matt told her it wasn't nice to discriminate against people who have disabilities." He drew Christy's head down till it rested against his chest.

"You know what I think?" Todd asked. "I think we all have disabilities or areas where we're impaired. You help me where I'm weak, and I help you where you're weak. That's what makes us strong together."

Christy wrapped her arms around his middle and cuddled up close. With a sigh she said, "I don't know, Todd. I hope you're right. Katie says I have a 'tidiness' issue. She says I have to have everything in place all the time or I'm not happy."

Todd chuckled.

"Do you think she's right?" Christy pulled back and looked into Todd's face.

"I think God brought us together so I could learn

the rewards of being spiritually disciplined from you and so you could learn the joys of walking by faith from me. We're made for each other, Kilikina."

Christy reached for Todd's hand and drew it to her lips. She kissed it three times. One kiss for each of the scars that remained after the near-fatal car accident he was in that fall.

"I hope you're right," she said.

"I am." Todd chuckled. He held her left hand and ran his rough fingers across the top of her long fingers. "Did you wish I had a ring for you when I proposed last night?"

"No."

"Are you sure? Because I asked my dad if I should buy a ring for you before I proposed. He said you probably would want to choose your own. Doug told me last night about a jeweler he likes here in Carlsbad. That's where he bought Tracy's ring. It's not far from here. I thought we could stop by this morning to see what they have."

Christy drew back and examined Todd's expression. "Is that why we came all the way to Carlsbad for breakfast burritos? You wanted to go ring shopping today?"

"Yeah." Todd grinned.

She closed her eyes and shook her head.

"What?"

"Todd, you know you can tell me these things ahead of time, don't you? I mean, it would have helped me to know that was why you wanted to drive down here."

"Okay, next time I'll tell you. See? We're learning to adjust already."

Todd helped her stand up, and they headed for the parking lot hand in hand. Christy felt herself warming up from the inside out as they drove into an older part of Carlsbad. She had fond memories of a jewelry store she and Todd had visited last summer when they were in Venice, Italy. It was owned by their friend's uncle and had to be the most elegant shop she had ever been in, complete with a uniformed guard at the door and gold chandeliers.

This Carlsbad jewelry store was located next to a bakery and a bookstore and didn't look nearly as opulent as the jewelry store in Venice. But what it lacked in golden chandeliers and uniformed guards it made up for in cozy ambience. Todd held open the door for Christy, and the fragrance of fresh-baked bread from the bakery next door swirled through the air.

Romantic visions of exchanging whisper-filled glances with Todd as she tried on engagement rings danced in Christy's head.

"Morning!" Todd greeted the gentleman at the back of the shop. "Is it okay if we look around?"

"Yes, of course. If I can answer any questions, please don't hesitate to ask. I'm Mr. Frank."

Christy felt like a princess as Todd motioned for her to take a seat at the padded bench in front of the first jewelry case. He stood behind her and, leaning over, pointed at the most noticeable ring in the center of the case. It had a large diamond in the center and three rubies on either side.

"Look at that one," Todd said.

"It's beautiful. But kind of big, don't you think? I like the smaller, simpler rings. Like that one." Christy pointed to a gold ring with a single diamond in a plain setting. "Only not that plain. I want my ring to be unique, you know?"

"Is there anything I can show you?" Mr. Frank came their way with a key in his hand.

"I'm not sure," Christy said quickly.

"Go ahead. Try it on," Todd said. "That way you'll know if you like the style or not."

Mr. Frank reached into the case for the padded velvet display box and took out the diamond solitaire. Christy slid the ring onto her left hand; it fit perfectly. The diamond was cut boldly and raised high on four prongs. She felt her hands begin to sweat. She had read the price on the attached tag when she slipped the ring on her finger and knew it must be an exceptional diamond. And she knew she could never feel comfortable wearing a ring that cost so much.

"What do you think?" Todd asked.

The phone rang, and Mr. Frank excused himself with a polite nod, leaving Christy and Todd alone for a few minutes. Todd leaned over and planted a kiss on Christy's unsuspecting lips.

With a chin-up gesture he asked again, "So, what do you think?"

Christy teasingly returned the chin-up gesture that

had been Todd's trademark for years and whispered, "I think you kiss pretty good."

Todd suppressed his laughter. With a finger to his lips he whispered, "I'm serious. What do you think?"

Christy blinked her eyes innocently and said, "I was serious, too. I think you kiss pretty good."

Todd reached over and tickled her. A burst of laughter almost escaped her lips, but she kept them pressed together until they hurt.

Mr. Frank finished his phone call. As he headed back toward them, Christy turned to Todd and whispered, "This ring is way too expensive."

Todd took her hand and turned it so he could read the price. "That's okay. If you like it, we can make payments. Don't let the price hold you back."

"It's not just the price, it's the ring. The style. I've never worn a lot of rings, but I know I'd like something smaller. Flatter. Something different."

"Different?" Todd questioned.

Mr. Frank stood before them and began to quote more facts about the diamond's clarity and size. "All of these rings are original designs made right here by my son and me."

Christy took the ring off her finger and tried to keep from giggling as she felt Todd's hand on her shoulder. If his fingers slipped behind her hair and started tickling her neck, she knew she would burst out laughing.

"Do you have anything different?" Todd asked in a controlled voice. "Anything flatter? And what did you say, Christy? Smaller?"

"Ah!" Mr. Frank seemed to enjoy the challenge set before him. "Something other than the traditional diamond. Perhaps a sapphire or a blue topaz, to match your lovely blue eyes. We have some particularly nice tanzanite."

For the next fifteen minutes, Todd refrained from tickling her as Christy tried on half a dozen non-diamond rings, with Mr. Frank giving a comprehensive lesson on each of the stones. With each ring she began to see potential options. Her imagination exploded with ideas when she tried on a particularly colorful Australian blue opal ring. The deep aqua blue stone with its flashes of green and purple reminded her of an ocean wave. And that reminded her of Todd and how they first had met at Newport Beach. However, the ring was too large, and the complicated setting didn't suit her.

"Do you have anything with this same sort of stone only in a smaller setting?" Christy asked. "Or even a flat setting like those bands with the diamond chips?"

"I don't believe we do. But as I mentioned earlier, we can make anything."

Christy was ready to design her ring right then and there. However, she glanced up at Todd before asking for paper and pencil. His expression was glazed over; he appeared to have reached his limit on looking for rings and learning the history of gemology.

"You've given us a lot to think about." Christy smiled at Mr. Frank. "I appreciate all your time."

"Allow me to present you with my card. If I may be

of any further assistance, please don't hesitate to call."

"Thank you," Christy said.

"Are you sure you don't want to try on any more rings?" Todd asked a little too politely.

Christy couldn't hold back her laughter any longer. She released a light giggle that floated on the air like a band of glistening soap bubbles. "I would love to, Todd, but I think I've already tried on every ring in the store."

They left with Todd's arm around her middle while he threatened to tickle her again.

"That poor man!" Christy exclaimed. "He kept looking at us like we weren't old enough to know what we were doing."

"I thought he was looking that way because he knew we didn't have enough money to buy anything but the peppermints in the dish by the register."

"Those were free," Christy said.

"They were? Hey, let's go back and get some." Todd turned around, but Christy grabbed his arm with both hands and pulled him toward the car. His comment about not having enough money sobered her.

"How are we going to pay for the rings and everything else?" she asked as soon as they were in the car.

"I have some money set aside," Todd said. He didn't start the engine but looked at her carefully. "It's not a lot, but my goal was to have enough for the ring, the tux, and the first three months of rent before I proposed. And I have that. Otherwise, I would have asked you to marry me a long time ago."

"You would have?"

Todd nodded. "I wanted us to get married before you went to Switzerland, but I knew that was an important year for you, and I didn't want to take it from you."

Christy thought a moment. "I don't think I would have been ready then. I don't even know if I'm ready now."

"Is that why you want a longer engagement?" Todd asked. "Do you need more time to be sure?"

"Oh, I'm sure I want to marry you." Christy reached for his hand and held it with both of hers. "I didn't mean that to sound the way it did. I'm sure with all my heart that I want to marry you. Only you. What I meant was I'm not sure I'm ready for all the adjustments and planning and decisions, like with the ring. I mean, you would think I would have an idea of what I want already, but I've never given it much thought. I just want it to be uniquely ours so that every time I look at it I'll think of us. Does that make sense?"

"Sure," Todd said. "You heard what he said. They can custom make anything you want. I'm sure you could have him put a stone like that blue one you liked into a different setting."

"It might take a while to do that," Christy said.

Todd flashed her a mischievous grin. "That's okay. It's not like we have to have the ring by January or anything."

Christy playfully thumped him on the arm. "Todd,

seriously, do you think we could pull off a wedding in less than a month?"

Todd shrugged. "Hey, all we need is a ring and a minister, right? And before you comment on that, how do you feel about stopping by to see Doug and Tracy?"

"Okay."

"Now, I like that answer." He started the car. "Quick, clean, decisive."

Christy settled back in her seat and thought about how much sense it made to wait until August for their wedding and about designing her own ring and about how much money they needed for rent. She thought about how many decisions they would need to make and how Todd appreciated "quick, clean, decisive" answers.

As Todd drove into a residential area where cottage-style beach bungalows lined the street, Christy came to a conclusion. "You know what, Todd? That's going to be my goal over the next few months. I'm going to work at making quick, clean decisions."

"You have good instincts, Christy. You should trust yourself and go with your gut feelings more often."

She studied his profile as he pulled up in front of Doug and Tracy's house. This man of her dreams who sat beside her had grown into a strong God-lover who was also deeply in love with her. Christy felt her heart pounding until she thought it would go *zing!* and fly right out of her.

"What?" Todd glanced at her as he backed their

Volvo into a space along the curb.

Christy pressed her lips together, intending to keep her zingy feelings inside. But then Todd stopped the car, looped his arm over the steering wheel, and turned to her with his silver-blue eyes peering deep into the secret place of her heart. Suddenly August seemed very far away.

"Okay," she said, following her gut instincts yet speaking in barely a whisper. "You win. January it is."

Todd leaned closer. "What did you say? I couldn't hear you."

Christy's heart raced. Her cheeks flushed. Never had she felt so overcome with the intensity of her love for Todd. Did she dare repeat the whispered words that had escaped her heart?

"What I said was . . ."

A flicker of an image came to Christy. The two of them were pulling away with a squeal from the very curb they had just parked in front of and driving one hundred miles an hour to the first drive-through wedding chapel they came to in Las Vegas.

She blinked. *No, this isn't one of those moments when I should trust my gut for a quick, clean decision. If I did, I'd end up dashing ahead of you and God and everyone else.*

"I said I love you," she whispered. "That's all."

"Oh, is that all?" Todd teased, pressing the back of his hand against her warm cheek. "Then why are you blushing?"

"Sunburn?" she ventured, raising her eyebrows and trying to look as innocent as possible.

"In December? I don't think so." Todd smiled at her. He seemed to be studying every detail of her face. His hand rose to the crown of her head. Gently, he stroked her long hair.

"Oh, Kilikina, if you only knew." He smoothed his thumb across her lips. "You have no idea what you and your love have brought to my life. You are the other half of my heart. Without you, my life would be only a shadow." He paused. "I love you, Kilikina. I love you more than you will ever know. More than you will ever ask. Nothing will ever change my love for you."

"Oh, Todd." Christy tilted her head toward him and offered him her lips.

Todd accepted her gift and kissed her slowly.

Just then a loud horn sounded in front of them, shattering their forever moment.

3 Todd and Christy reluctantly drew away from each other and looked through the car's windshield. They saw Doug pulling his truck into his narrow driveway, wildly waving at them. Jumping out of his yellow truck, he came over to Todd's open window and said, "Hey, did I just catch you two making out in front of my house?"

"We weren't making out." Christy felt her face turn red all over again.

Doug laughed. His face lit up with a little-boy expression that had become familiar to Christy over the years. Doug was taller than Todd, but with his short, blond hair and mischievous grin, he could have passed for a high school freshman. "I suppose you're going to tell me Todd was checking your hair to see if it smelled like green apples."

"No, that's your line, Doug." Todd glanced at Christy with an equally charming little-boy grin and stated matter-of-factly, "We were kissing." He pressed the back of his fingers against Christy's cheeks. "This is

my blushing bride. We're going to get married. Did you
know that, Doug?"

Doug punched Todd in the arm. "The whole world
knows it after last night. You two space cadets better
come in and see everyone. Tracy will be thrilled you're
here. We had a big sleepover last night. Rick is going to
make omelets."

"Rick?"

"Yeah, Rick's here. It's been awesome hearing what
God has done in his life. He and Katie had us laughing
all night."

"Katie?"

"Yeah, Katie is here, too. So were Sierra, Paul, Vicki,
and Wes." Doug opened Todd's door. "You two want to
help me carry in the groceries? I had to make a run for
supplies."

"That explains what happened to my roomie last
night," Christy said.

Todd and Christy followed Doug to the front door,
each carrying two bags of groceries. Doug and Tracy's
cozy cottage was four blocks from the beach and was
the only yellow house with white shutters on their
street. It had one bedroom and one bathroom. The living room area opened into the kitchen, and they had a
small backyard, where Tracy had worked hard to start
a flower garden.

As soon as they entered, Katie leaped from the
couch and met Christy with a huge hug. "Did you get
my message? Why didn't you come last night? We had
a great time celebrating your engagement. You should

have been here. When I called you late last night the line was busy."

Katie seemed even more energetic than usual.

"I was talking to my parents," Christy said.

Taking one of the grocery bags from Christy, Katie asked, "Were they surprised about your engagement?"

"No. Todd talked to my dad earlier and asked for my parents' blessing."

"It was more like asking his permission," Todd said.

"Permission or blessing," Christy said. "My dad gave both. My parents were waiting for me to call. They're thrilled. My mom cried. Then I called my aunt and uncle."

"Did they know Todd was going to propose last night?"

"No, but they weren't surprised. They're real happy for us, too." Christy stepped into the kitchen area of Doug and Tracy's compact house and received a warm grin from Rick.

"We're all real happy for you." Rick reached in front of Katie and offered Todd a handshake. "You two have a great future ahead of you."

Christy noticed that although Rick was still his tall, dark, and handsome self, he didn't seem to wear an attitude of arrogance like a prince's crown, which is what he had done when he was in high school. Standing next to Katie in Doug and Tracy's homey kitchen, Rick appeared average. Katie's flashing green eyes and soft, distinctive new look with her short, feathery red hair made her the first person Christy's eyes went to.

"Where's everyone else?" Doug asked, unloading the bountiful groceries.

"Tracy is in the shower; Paul had to go to work; Sierra, Wes, and Vicki had to get back to school because they're driving home to Oregon for Christmas break." Katie's expression lit up another couple of watts as she turned to Christy. "I wish you guys had come last night. We stayed up all night talking. It was awesome."

"Uh-oh." Rick gave Katie a playful tag on the arm. "You've been around Doug too long. You're starting to say 'awesome.' "

"Well, it was an awesome time for all of us last night. You guys would have loved it. We laughed so hard!" Katie began to recount the previous night's events while Christy moved to the living room and lowered herself into the chair beside the couch. Katie looked radiant as she spoke with charming animation. What an improvement over the way Katie looked twenty-four hours earlier when the gang was planning to go to The Dove's Nest. Katie had proclaimed she would rather stay alone in their dorm room since she didn't have a date. That was before Rick stepped into the center of their group.

Christy thought back on the way she had fallen for Rick in high school. Katie had a huge crush on him, too. But Christy got over Rick pretty fast; Katie never seemed to have recovered. Katie's love for Rick had turned to anger and simmered deep and low within her for years.

Then a few months ago a letter from Rick arrived.

He told Katie how he had completely turned his life over to the Lord, and he asked Katie for her forgiveness for the way he had treated her in the past.

From the way she's looking at him right now, I would say Katie has forgiven Rick completely.

"Hey, Todd," Doug said after Katie concluded her entertaining summary. "I need to check on Tracy real quick, and then I need your help on something. I've been working on a song, and these guys helped me last night, but I can't get one part in the chorus right."

"Do you want us to start the omelets?" Katie called out as Doug headed for the bedroom.

"Sure," Doug said. "Go ahead."

"Do you know where they keep their cheese grater?" Rick asked.

"Try the cupboard on your right," Katie suggested.

"Anything I can do to help?" Christy asked.

"Sure," Rick said. "You can find a mixing bowl larger than this one."

"I think Tracy keeps those over here." Christy opened a cupboard as Katie's spontaneous laughter came rolling over her. Whenever Katie got going with her most joyful strain of laughter, others found it nearly impossible to keep a straight face. Her laughter carried the sound of glee at its freest, happiest, lightest moment and tickled all those who heard it.

Christy turned around and saw Katie holding up a couple of aprons she had found in a drawer. "This one is for you," Katie said to Rick. "And this one is mine."

Rick tied a frilly yellow apron trimmed with pastel

flowers around his waist. It barely fit. Katie laughed again. Echoing Katie's winged laughter came the bass notes of a concert of mirth from Rick. It was a richer and more genuine laugh than Christy had ever heard spill from him.

Katie's apron was denim with stripes. Across the bib were the words *File All Complaints Here.* An arrow pointed to a tiny pocket that wouldn't hold many complaints.

"Trade you," Rick said.

"Not a chance."

Christy placed the large mixing bowl on the counter. "Anything else I can do?"

"We need plates," Rick said. "Can you find six dinner plates?"

The cupboard was empty, so Christy unloaded the clean dishes from the dishwasher while Rick and Katie went to work. Within a few moments, it appeared that they had turned the kitchen into a quirky cable cooking show. They had mushrooms cooking in a small frying pan and sausage going in a larger pan. Bowls and various cooking tools were scattered everywhere.

"We'll make an assembly line so everyone can custom-order their omelets," Rick explained. "If you want, Christy, you can grate the cheese."

Christy took her project over to the kitchen table to get out of the way. With amazement she watched the marvel of Rick and Katie, working side by side as if they had practiced the steps to this kitchen dance for years.

Todd strummed Doug's guitar as he sat on the living room couch. Christy didn't recognize the tune he was playing. She wondered if that was the song he had been working on last night.

Then, as if Todd felt her gaze on him, he looked over at her. A slow smile played on his lips. He kept strumming and then mouthed a word she didn't catch.

Christy gave him a look indicating she didn't understand him.

Todd mouthed the word again. "January."

Christy broke into a smile as bright as the sunrise. *You heard me in the car, didn't you, Todd? You heard me whisper "January" to you. Well, I know we can't pull off a wedding in January, but maybe we can pull it off by February. We could get married right after you graduate. I'd only have one more semester to go and—*

Doug stepped into the living room, blocking Christy's view of Todd.

What am I thinking? February is too soon. We can wait until this summer, can't we?

Doug began to play his new song. Christy pulled her thoughts back to the present. She felt a comforting sense of warmth come over her as Doug's familiar voice filled the cozy home where these good friends gathered.

> "When the Lord brought us together
> We were like those who dreamed
> Our mouths were filled with laughter
> Our tongues with songs of joy.
> Then it was said
> The Lord has done great things for them

Yes, the Lord has done great things for us
And we are filled with joy."

"Isn't that a great song?" Katie asked.

"What Scripture did you base it on?" Todd asked.

"Psalm 126," Doug said. "And this is the problem, here on this line. How do I make the transition from 'When the Lord brought us together' to 'We were like those who dreamed'? It isn't smooth."

Christy stopped grating the cheese. *Boy, that was a true statement, Doug. You don't realize it, but that's the question I've been struggling with all day. How do two dreamers make a smooth transition when the Lord brings them together?*

She wished he would play the whole song again. She wanted to hear the part about the Lord doing great things and about being filled with joy.

Just then the bathroom door opened, and petite Tracy stepped out with a huge smile on her heart-shaped face. "Hi!" she greeted Todd and Christy.

"Hey, how's it goin'?" Todd greeted her with a chin-up nod.

Christy rose and went over to give Tracy a hug. As soon as their arms went around each other, Tracy whispered in Christy's ear, "Guess what? I'm pregnant!"

"What?!" Christy squealed, pulling back and looking at Tracy's face to be sure she had heard right.

"Trace," Doug scolded, "did you tell her?"

"Tell her what?" Katie asked from the kitchen.

All eyes were on Tracy.

"We were going to wait until we sat down to eat." Doug handed Todd the guitar and went over to his wife, who was standing next to Christy and biting her lower lip.

"I'm sorry, honey! I didn't mean to say anything. It just flew right out of my mouth," Tracy confessed.

Doug put his arm around her and gave her a look of unfaltering devotion. "Go ahead, sweetheart. Tell everybody."

"You," she said.

"Oh, now you've turned shy." Doug laughed and gave his wife a big hug. "It looks like the Lord has decided to bless us with a baby."

A cheer rose from the group. They all took turns hugging and congratulating Doug and Tracy.

Todd crossed the room in four steps and slipped his arm around Christy. He kissed the side of her head, above her right ear. She knew he was thinking the same thing she was thinking. One day, Lord willing, they would be the ones making a similar announcement to their friends.

"Is something burning?" Tracy sniffed the air.

"It's the olive oil in the pan." Rick jogged back to the stove. "I'll turn it down."

"Could you open the window above the kitchen sink?" Tracy asked.

"Morning sickness," Doug explained. "She's not real steady until about two in the afternoon. She's sensitive to strong scents."

"When is the baby due?" Christy asked.

"July, according to our calculations," Tracy said. "We'll find out more after my appointment with the doctor next week."

"When did you guys find out?" Katie asked.

"Yesterday morning. It's been torture keeping it a secret from you guys, but we agreed we wanted to tell our parents first, and we weren't able to get ahold of them on the phone until this morning, right before Doug went for the groceries."

"I can't believe you didn't say anything last night," Katie said.

"Last night was Todd and Christy's night." Tracy sent Christy a gentle smile.

"Yeah, one major announcement at a time is about all this group can handle," Doug added.

"Don't worry about me!" Katie said. "I don't have any announcements or secrets this morning."

A crazy thought flitted through Christy's mind. She wondered if Katie would soon be announcing that Rick had asked her out. Christy shooed away the notion. It was far too early for that. Or maybe it was far too late, since they had already given that a try in high school.

Doug kissed his wife soundly. "We're open to suggestions on names because so far we haven't agreed on any names for boys or girls."

After a round of suggestions, none of which struck a chord with the happy couple, Doug returned to the couch with Todd to work on the song.

"Do you have a fan on this stove?" Rick asked. "I can't seem to find one."

"It's broken," Doug said.

"Is the smell still too strong for you, Tracy?" Rick said.

"No, it's okay." Tracy opened the front door to let in more air. "This will help. So, Rick, when did you become such a gourmet chef?"

Christy thought Tracy's redirection of the conversation was so typical of her. She didn't like having the attention on herself. Tracy seemed most comfortable when she was listening to her friends or offering them kind advice. Christy had a long list of questions to ask Tracy about her engagement and wedding details, but she decided to wait until the two of them could be alone.

"Cooking is one of my hidden talents," Rick replied to Tracy's question.

"I don't remember hearing about your cooking much when you and Doug and Todd shared the apartment in San Diego," Tracy said.

Rick laughed. "That's because we never had any food in our apartment!"

"You got that right," Todd said.

"Amen!" Doug agreed.

"I learned a few things at the restaurant where I worked."

"The Blue Parachute," Katie said.

Rick looked surprised. "That's right. How did you know that, Katie?"

"We went there one night after the Bible study at your apartment, remember? Christy and I came down to San Diego, and you were at the hospital when we arrived because you sprained your wrist."

"Oh yeah, that's right." Rick seemed to be having a hard time remembering that night. "You guys came down, and we went to the zoo."

Christy remembered the experience vividly because she had watched Rick kiss Katie the night of the Bible study. The next day at the zoo Rick treated Katie terribly. He acted as if nothing had happened between them the night before.

Standing only a few feet from Katie, Christy watched her expression. She saw no indication on Katie's face that the memory of Rick and the zoo was still painful.

"My mom is the real cook in our family," Rick said. "That's how my dad came up with the idea of starting The Dove's Nest Café next to the Christian bookstore."

"Why did your dad build The Dove's Nest and The Ark out in Murietta Hot Springs instead of where they live in Escondido or here at the beach?" Doug asked.

"He got a great deal on the property in Murietta. It would have cost two or three times as much here."

Katie turned to Christy. "And guess where I'm going to work starting in January?"

"Let me guess. The car wash in Temecula?"

"Nooo," Katie answered playfully. "Guess again. It starts with a 'dove' and ends with a 'nest.' "

"Wait a minute," Christy said. "I thought you said you didn't have any big announcements or secrets?"

"This isn't exactly a secret," Rick said. "We've been looking for people who can work evenings. It's entry level, but I have a feeling she'll work her way up to just about any position she wants."

Christy studied her best friend even more carefully. "And just what position do you want, Miss Katie?"

"To attend the Natural Food Faire in San Diego."

Christy hadn't expected an answer, especially such a random one.

"It's held every February. Rick says we can go and introduce my new Indian Summer herbal tea."

Christy took note of her roommate's answer. Katie had said "we." That meant Katie and Rick. The two of them were planning to go together. And the fair wasn't until February.

"Are you ready for this?" Rick asked Christy.

No, I'm not ready for Katie and you to be making plans together so naturally, Rick Doyle. Katie may have forgiven you for the way you treated her years ago, but you're going to have to prove to me you're worthy of renewing such a chummy relationship with my best friend.

Rick pointed to the frying pan and repeated his question. "Are you ready for me to make your omelet? Tell me what you want in it."

"Oh. Just some cheese."

"Is that all?"

Christy nodded.

"Don't worry," Katie said. "My omelet will allow you to showcase your culinary skills."

"That's my girl." Rick flashed Katie a big smile. He didn't say it with the manipulative edge his voice had carried in high school. His words, his tone, his expression all reflected warm genuineness.

And it gave Christy a shiver up her spine. *Katie, girl, you and I need to talk.*

CHRISTY AND TODD · THE COLLEGE YEARS

The opportunity for Christy to have a heart-to-heart discussion with Katie seemed to present itself late that night when Katie finally returned to their dorm room. Christy was busy packing her things to go home for Christmas vacation as Katie burst in, bright as a sunbeam.

"Hello, favorite of all the roomies in all the world! Is God incredible or what?" Katie twirled around and flopped on her unmade bed. "I'm telling you, Chris, life is never dull when God is doing His God-things. I'm speechless. No, I'm overly full of speech. Full of praise, actually."

Katie jumped up and dashed across the room to tackle Christy in a hug. "And speaking of miracles, I still can't believe you and Todd finally are engaged! I loved watching you two sitting close on the couch at Doug and Tracy's. It was adorable the way you were sharing bites of each other's omelets. You both looked so happy, and by the way, weren't those great omelets? Is Rick amazing or what?"

"Katie!" Christy laughed and grasped her friend firmly by the shoulders. "Take a breath! I've seen you hyper before but never this hyper. How much caffeine have you had today?"

"I don't know. Enough to keep me awake after staying up all night. And I drank a lot of homemade hot chocolate. Todd and you left before Rick made it. I had three mugsful! You should have stayed; it was so good. Did you guys go to the mall?" Katie flitted over to her dresser and began to pull out clothes and cosmetics and toss them on her bed.

"No. We were going to look at more rings, but we ended up talking for a long time, and then Todd dropped me off here so I could take a nap before we went to dinner."

"You wouldn't have needed a nap if you had had some of this hot chocolate! You know how they say that chocolate can give you the feeling of being in love?" Katie wagged her toothbrush at Christy. "Well, I never believed it before today, but after three mugs of pure chocolate, I'm definitely in love!"

"In love with chocolate?" Christy ventured.

"No, not in love with chocolate. In love, in love. You know. Really in love." Katie's green eyes sparkled as she stopped long enough to give Christy a sideways glance. "Do you think that could be possible?"

Christy wasn't sure she was following Katie's logic. "Are you asking if it's possible for you to be in love someday?"

"Yes, but not someday. Today. With Rick." Katie's

face went red. "Do you suppose I'm really, truly, finally in love?"

"Katie, it would make more sense if—"

"I know, I know." Katie turned on her heel and pulled out a large gym bag from her closet. "I'm just hyper. It must be the hot chocolate high. Rick used dark chocolate. I think there's a difference." She tossed a pair of shoes into the bag and a crumpled pair of jeans. "Dark chocolate probably has more caffeine. Or more of that stuff that induces feelings of being in love."

"Maybe," Christy answered cautiously. Then in an effort to move the conversation to a neutral topic so Katie would come down a notch, Christy said, "Are you going to drive home in the morning?"

"No, I'm going home tonight. Didn't I tell you?" Katie paused and added, "Rick is taking me. He's waiting in the lobby. Oh, and I almost forgot. He said he wanted to talk to you if you were here."

"He wants to talk to me? What about?"

Katie shrugged.

"So, if Rick is driving you home, are you leaving your car here during Christmas break?" Christy asked, trying to make sense of Katie's last-minute plans.

"No. See, I drove Baby Hummer home last night after your engagement party. Rick followed me, and then he and I drove to Doug and Tracy's since their house is only twenty minutes from my parents' house."

Christy nodded.

"Then, when we left Doug and Tracy's this afternoon, we went to the movies. Then Rick drove me
back here to pick up my stuff. Now we're going to Escondido." Katie casually flipped a feathery strand of
hair off her forehead as if her suddenly exploding social life made complete sense.

"Katie?" Christy asked in a small voice.

Katie either didn't hear her or chose not to hear as
she continued to haphazardly toss things into her bag
and kept talking. "Oh, and I should tell you, Rick
wants to go to Mexico with us next week, so we need
to add one more to the list when we go buy the food.
He said he would help us cook when we're down
there. He suggested spaghetti."

"Katie . . ."

"I told him you probably had the grocery list already figured out. If you'd like, I could ask him to go
shopping with us. I'm sure Rick would—"

"Katie!"

"What?" Katie turned and faced Christy, and when
she did, her entire countenance fell. "Oh no you don't.
I know that look." Katie set her jaw and lowered her
chin.

"What look?"

"I know exactly what you're going to say to me."

Christy laughed nervously. She hadn't thought she
was that transparent. Her concern for Katie obviously
showed all over her face.

Katie put down the gym bag and crossed the room
in three steps. "You're going to ask me if I've thought

this through and if I think that spending all this time with Rick is a good idea."

"Well . . ." Christy hesitated. Katie was exactly right, but Christy didn't want to admit it.

"And you know what?" Katie planted her hands on her hips. "I won't let you ask me those questions right now because I didn't go looking for this, Christy. You know I didn't. It just happened. Rick was there at The Dove's Nest, and the guys tried to play a joke on me by having Rick come over and ask me out. But the joke is . . ." Katie's eyes brimmed with tears, and her voice quavered. "The joke is that it isn't a joke. This is the most wonderful, amazing thing that has ever happened to me, Christy Miller, and you are *not* going to analyze it away from me!"

Christy swallowed all the sisterly words of caution that had been filling her mouth. She kept her lips together, not daring to let out a single sound.

"Thank you." Katie turned with her head held high. "Thank you, my best friend. That's the nicest gift you could give me at this moment." She grabbed her bag and motioned with her head for Christy to follow her. "Come on, Rick wanted to talk to you, remember?"

Christy followed quietly, wondering if she was doing the right thing to keep her apprehensions to herself.

In the middle of the dorm hallway, Katie said, "If this is a God-thing, it will last. If not, it will dissolve. I know that because I've never been so completely open to God's leading in my life as I am right now. I think it's the same for Rick. Neither of us is trying to make this happen. It's just what it is, and it will be whatever it's going to be."

Christy nodded her agreement, and a surprising calm came over her. For some reason she thought of how her aunt had always tried to control Christy's social life and how much Christy disliked it when Aunt Marti interfered. If it had been Aunt Marti's choice, Christy would never have developed her friendship with Katie. But what did Aunt Marti know?

The last thing I want to do is to take on my aunt's controlling characteristics!

"I love you, Katie," Christy said just before they walked into the lobby.

Katie flashed Christy a smile. "I love you, too."

"Hey, Christy," Rick said as they strode toward him. "I have something I wanted to give you. I was going to mail this." He pulled an envelope from his back pocket. "But I hoped to somehow be able to hand it to you. I guess this is the opportunity I was hoping for."

"Would you like me to leave you guys alone?" Katie asked.

"No, I don't mind if you hear this, Katie. I mean, if Christy doesn't mind."

"No, it's fine."

"I guess you both know I've been trying to make things right with people I hurt in the past and . . ." Rick seemed to have run out of words. He held out the crumpled envelope to Christy.

"Rick," Christy felt as nervous as he looked at this

moment, "you don't need to apologize to me for anything. You and I settled everything a long time ago. I
don't—"

"We didn't exactly settle everything," Rick said. "I,
uh, I did something really cruel and foolish when . . .
well, you know . . ." He drew in a deep breath. "When
you and I were dating, Christy, I stole your bracelet. Or
rather, Todd's bracelet. Or, I mean, the bracelet Todd
gave you."

Christy bit the inside of her lower lip. She knew she
had forgiven Rick for that long ago, but watching him
so tortured as he made his confession to her brought
all the emotions back to the surface for her, as well.

"I'm very sorry, Christy. That was wrong. I know
you've forgiven me. But I also know that Doug and you
made payments on the bracelet to the jewelry store
where I traded it in."

Christy noticed that Rick's forehead was glistening
with perspiration as he continued. "I've made things
right with Doug, and now I'd like to make things right
with you. Christy, please accept this with my apology."
Rick's deep brown eyes begged for forgiveness.

"Thank you, Rick. I already forgave you, like you
said."

"But you'll keep what's in that envelope," Rick said.
"Promise me you'll keep it."

"Okay, I promise. Thank you."

Rick nodded. He looked relieved.

"I, um . . ." Christy felt another wave of awkward-
ness come over her. She didn't want to open the enve-

lope in front of Rick and Katie, and she didn't want to prolong the conversation. "I guess I shouldn't hold you two up. You have a long drive ahead of you."

"Yeah, I guess we should get going." Rick reached for Katie's gym bag and backpack. "Is this all you have?"

"Yep," Katie said. "I travel light these days, thanks to my best friend's influence. Christy taught me all about traveling light when we were in Europe."

"I want to hear more about your trip," Rick said. "You guys went to Italy, right?"

"Yes."

"Did you go to the island of Capri?"

"Yes." Katie seemed to anticipate his next question. "And yes, we went to the Blue Grotto that you are so crazy about."

"You did?" Rick's expression lit up.

"Yes," Katie said with a grin at Christy. "Christy and Todd loved it, but I thought it was dark and cold and highly overrated. I mean, if you think about it, it's just a dark cave with water and a bunch of men wearing straw hats and singing loudly in Italian."

Rick's mouth dropped open.

Christy laughed. *Rick, I'd say you just had a full dose of the real Katie.*

Regaining his composure, Rick said, "You know, you're right, Katie. It is just a dark cave with water and singing Italian boatmen. I guess it's who you're with in the dark cave that makes it romantic."

"Oh, you want to talk romantic," Katie said, head-ing for the door, "then let's talk about Venice. I loved Venice. When you were there, did you go for a ride in a gondola? Now, that's a boat ride with a view."

"You guys went for a gondola ride?" Rick followed Katie to the door.

As Katie recounted the details of their adventure, Rick turned and gave Christy a warm smile. "See you later."

"I'll give you a call tomorrow." Katie waved over her shoulder. "You're going home after church, aren't you?"

Christy nodded.

"I'll call you," Katie said.

Christy waved. "Bye, you guys. Drive safely."

Turning to go back to her room, Christy chided herself. *Drive safely? Why am I talking like their mother would?*

Once Christy was back in the solitude of her dorm room, she reached for the phone and dialed Todd's number. She could tell from the sound in his voice that she had awakened him, but she asked the obvious anyway. "Were you asleep?"

"That's okay. What's up? Are you all right?"

Christy summarized her conversations with Katie and Rick. But before she could mention Rick's envelope, Todd said, "That's how it is when God's working in our lives. We always need to save room for the unexpected."

Christy thought of how Todd's life seemed to have plenty of room for the unexpected. He even seemed to look for the unexpected, like when he took breakfast to the homeless man that morning.

"I don't do that very well," Christy said. "I don't leave room on my calendar or in my daily schedule for God to do unexpected things."

"That's okay," Todd said. "I have a pretty good idea God will keep finding ways to fit them into your life anyway."

"God sure did that tonight." Christy told Todd about the envelope Rick had given her.

"You haven't opened it yet?" Todd asked.

"No, I don't know if I want to. In a way, I just want to throw it away and let it be over."

"Didn't you say Rick asked you to promise to keep it?"

"That's right, he did."

"You don't have to open it now," Todd said. "And you don't have to tell me what's in it when you open it. But you do have to honor your promise to Rick."

"You're right," Christy said quietly. "And I will. I think the best thing for now would be if I went to bed and got some sleep."

"Good idea. I'll see you in the morning."

"Good night, my Todd."

"Good night, my Kilikina. I love you."

"And I love you."

A settled calm came over Christy and over the dorm room after she hung up. She sat in the silence and stared at the envelope in her hand. Rick had written her first name in small, cursive letters. From the wear and tear on the envelope, he had been carrying it with him for some time.

Putting aside the envelope, Christy packed her neatly folded clothes that were still sitting on her bed. Right before she pulled down the covers, she reached for Rick's envelope and tucked it into her suitcase's side pocket.

The next day after church, as she and Todd drove home to Escondido, she thought again of the envelope. She wasn't sure why she hadn't opened it the night before. She should have opened it while she was talking to Todd on the phone so the entire incident could have been concluded. She knew Todd would never ask her about it.

When I get home, I'll open the envelope, show the contents to Todd, and it will be over. Settled. We'll all be able to move forward. I don't know why I'm being so squirmy about this. It's probably a letter of apology like the one he sent Katie.

What Christy hadn't anticipated was that Aunt Marti and Uncle Bob would be at her parents' house when she and Todd arrived.

"We couldn't wait until Christmas at our house to see you two." Marti kissed Christy on both cheeks and then turned her affectionate attentions toward Todd.

Marti had gone through a lot of personal changes during the past year. In September, she had arrived at Rancho to take Christy out to lunch. But after seeing Aunt Marti, Christy and Katie had concluded Marti already was "out to lunch." Her hair extensions, minimal makeup, and long, flowing gauze skirt, along with an announcement that she was considering going to Santa Fe with her new pottery instructor, served as all the proof Christy and Katie needed.

But Marti hadn't gone to Santa Fe. She and Uncle Bob seemed to be working on their relationship. And Marti's dark hair was cut in a short crop that framed her face in a softened style. Even Marti's perfume smelled like a fragrance Christy remembered from years ago.

Uncle Bob gave Christy a hug, and she noticed his dark hair was going gray by his ears. Bob and Todd both had been burned several years ago when Bob's gas grill went haywire and exploded. The black turtle-neck Bob was wearing hid the scars on his neck.

Christy smiled at her patient uncle and wondered how his scars on the inside were doing, the scars from the hurts he must have suffered while Aunt Marti was going through her mid-life crisis.

Christy hugged her mom and dad, and then Marti jumped in and said she was ready to discuss wedding plans.

"I'll be back in a minute." Christy excused herself from the clutch of family members in the living room and carried her suitcase into her bedroom at the end of the hall. Closing the door, she leaned her back against it and swallowed hard.

Marti always had delighted in a project. Could it be that Todd and Christy's wedding was her latest grand event? Why hadn't Christy seen this coming? It made her clench her teeth to think of her aunt elbowing her way into Todd and Christy's plans and trying to take over. Yet, at the same time, Christy knew that as long as Marti had a project that kept her in Newport Beach with her husband, she was less likely to run off to join her new friends at their art colony in New Mexico.

A tap on the door made Christy jump. "Who is it?"

"It's me, David. Can I come in?"

Christy opened the door to let her fifteen-year-old brother into her private enclave. "Hi. How are you?" She gave him a quick hug, since he never had been a big fan of snuggling.

"Mom said you're getting married." David had passed up Christy's five-foot-seven-inch frame some time ago, but now he was filling out across the shoulders. His hair had always had more of their father's red tones than Christy's, but now it carried a stronger hue of blond, and Christy was stunned at how much older he looked.

"Where are your glasses?" Christy asked.

"Didn't Mom tell you? I broke my glasses twice this year while skateboarding. I told Mom and Dad all I wanted for Christmas was contacts. I got them yesterday, and Mom said I could start wearing them because I wanted to get used to them during the school break."

"Look at you. David, you are so grown-up. You're cute. No, you're handsome." Christy gave her brother a big smile. "David, you are adorable!"

David cracked a slight grin. "I'm glad you aren't one of those people who judge others simply by their outward appearance."

Christy laughed. "And a sense of humor, too! David, when did you get so cool?"

"I've always been cool, Christy."

She laughed and gave him another hug even though he didn't seem comfortable with all her gushing and squeezing.

"Did Mom tell you I joined a Christian club for skaters?"

"No." Christy flopped on her bed. "Where do they meet?"

"You make it sound like we have a clubhouse or something." David leaned against the closed door. "We just hang out at the skate park. This guy from our church comes every Thursday afternoon at four-thirty, and some of us sit down with him, and he has a Bible study. I'm learning a lot."

"Do you have a good Bible?" Christy had been with David when he gave his life to the Lord while Todd was in the hospital, but she realized she hadn't done much to follow up with him. She knew he was going to church with her parents, and this skaters' Bible study was good to hear about. But since she didn't have a Christmas present for him yet, a Bible sounded like a good idea.

"No."

"Do you want one?" Christy asked.

"I guess. I mean, I have a kid's version I got when I was like eight, but it has pictures, and I don't want to take that one to the skate park."

Christy remembered when she got her first "real"

Bible. Todd and Tracy gave it to her for her fifteenth birthday. At the time, she hadn't appreciated it. She decided then that she would buy David a contemporary version for Christmas, but she would buy him something else, too.

"So are you guys really getting married?" David asked again.

"Yes." Christy's grin broadened. She kicked off her shoes and folded her legs under her, settling comfortably onto her old bed.

"When?"

"We haven't decided yet."

"Mom says it probably won't be for another year."

"A year?" Christy questioned.

"But Aunt Marti says it will be in June."

"Oh, she does, does she?" Christy leaned forward. "And what does Dad say?"

"Nothing. He just listens. Mom and Aunt Marti almost got into an argument before you came. Aunt Marti says you have to have the reception at some boat club in Newport Beach, and Mom says it's going to be at the church."

Christy shook her head.

"What do Todd and you want?" David looked more sensitive and interested in her life than he ever had before.

A slow, appreciative smile grew as Christy said, "David, you might be the only one here today to ask me that question. So will you do me a favor and ask it again in front of everyone else?"

"Okay." David appeared not to see why it was a big deal. "I mean, it's your wedding, right? It's your life. You should do what you want. You guys have been waiting a long time."

"Yes, we have."

They were quiet for a few moments. Through Christy's closed bedroom door, she could hear Aunt Marti's voice rising as she shared her wedding insights with poor Todd.

"I guess I should go back out there and support my fiancé," she said.

"Todd's okay," David said. "He won't let Aunt Marti push him around."

Christy wished she had as much confidence as her brother on the subject. She stood and headed for the door. David didn't budge. Christy looked at him with questioning eyes.

David looked away shyly. "I don't know what the right word is, but whatever you're supposed to say when somebody gets engaged, I guess . . . well, I'm happy for you guys. I'm glad you're getting married."

Impulsively leaning forward, Christy kissed her brother on the cheek. "Thank you, David. I love you."

He stiffened up as his face turned pink. "Yeah, me too."

With her heart light, Christy opened her bedroom door and went forward to meet her formidable aunt. Her embarrassed baby brother lumbered down the hall behind her.

"There you are," Marti said when Christy and David entered the living room.

5 Todd was wedged in the middle of the couch with Marti on one side and Christy's mom on the other. On his lap was a stack of bridal magazines. Christy would have burst out laughing if it weren't for the shocked look on Todd's face. If he was going to figure out how much detailed planning went into a wedding, it would be here and now.

"I was just telling Todd we had the photos Bob took of you two at Thanksgiving developed and then sent copies of the best one into our newspaper's society section as well as yours," Marti said. "They'll appear this weekend. Oh, and I took the liberty to write a little story about your engagement."

"That was fast," Christy said.

"It's perfect timing, really, this weekend being Christmas and all. I didn't want to miss the opportunity to get it in there in time."

Christy nodded and gave Todd an encouraging grin.

"I'm getting a drink of water. Anyone else want anything?"

"Sure," Todd's voice squeaked out.

Christy had to smile again. *My poor Todd. I don't think he's ready for this. But I do know that the reality check will be good for him.*

She walked toward the kitchen, where she could hear her dad and Uncle Bob talking.

"You're not leaving us, are you, Christina?" Marti called out. "I've barely begun to go over the details here."

"I'll be right back."

"I only have one question for you to answer," her dad said as Christy reached for two glasses from the cupboard. "Have Todd and you discussed a wedding date?"

"The sooner the better." Uncle Bob raised his bottle of mineral water in a mock toast.

"Have you been talking to Todd?" Christy asked her uncle as she filled the glasses with ice.

"No, not yet. But I'll tell him the same thing I'm telling you, which is what I was just telling your dad. Don't let finances hold you back. Martha and I would love to help out on that end."

"Your mother thinks you should wait until next Christmas," Christy's dad said.

"So I heard. What do you think, Dad?"

He was a large, quiet man who tended to hold his comments until he had time to think them through.

His expression told Christy he was honored she had asked his opinion.

"Well, you know how I feel about your having the privilege of getting a college education. Neither your mother nor I had that opportunity."

"I know," Christy said. "I agree. I told Todd we should wait until I graduate."

"You're so close to being finished," Bob said. "I don't see why you couldn't complete your final semester after the wedding. You could even skip this next semester, get married after Todd graduates in January, and then go back in the fall."

"Hello in there!" Marti called from the living room. "We're waiting out here. You three aren't discussing wedding plans without me, are you?"

"Yes," Christy called out brashly.

Her uncle grinned and toasted her again. "Go get 'em, bright eyes!"

Christy motioned with her head for her dad and uncle to follow her as she carried the two glasses of water back to the living room and handed one to Todd. "Come on. You two should be in on this."

"Sit over here." Marti handed Christy a thick bridal magazine and pointed to a picture of a model in a wedding dress with a full skirt. "I was glancing at this on our drive down here, and I wondered if you had considered this sort of veil. I'm assuming you'll be wearing your hair up and back to show off your face."

Christy placed the magazine on the floor. She smiled at Todd. "I'm going to wear flowers in my hair."

Todd smiled back at her. His expression of frozen panic began to melt.

"I don't see why you couldn't add some flowers to the connecting headpiece of this veil." Marti retrieved the magazine and studied the picture.

"Aunt Marti, we're not ready to talk about those kinds of details."

Marti looked up at Christy. "You're right. First things first. Todd tells me you've begun to look at rings but haven't made a decision yet. I'm sure you know that you'll be hard pressed to size the ring in time for Christmas. But it can be done, if you make your selection today. Tomorrow morning at the latest, I would imagine. I'm assuming you're going to get your ring for Christmas."

"Martha," Uncle Bob said firmly, "let the kids take it at their own pace. You said on the way here that you wanted to listen to them and let them tell you where they wanted us to help out. I think we better let them do the talking here."

Marti pulled back. She seemed to take Bob's reproof better than Christy would have guessed. "Yes. Of course. Fine. Go ahead. Tell us your plans. All we know so far is that you haven't decided on a ring. Or a date. Or any of the other essentials." Aunt Marti glanced at Christy's mom and in a lower voice added, "But she knows she's going to wear flowers in her hair."

Christy felt a familiar mixture of anger and pain rising inside. She knew she should ignore the barb. That's what the others in the room seemed to do automatically.

"Why don't we start with the date," Bob suggested. "Todd, I was telling Christy and Norm that the wedding's expense shouldn't hold the two of you back. You know that Marti and I would be honored to help out in that area."

"What about school?" Christy's mom looked concerned.

Marti jumped in. "You do know that most reservations need to be made a year ahead of time for your reception to be held at, say, the Newport Bay Yacht Club. And a custom-made dress can take at least six months, sometimes nine, depending on how many fittings you need."

Christy noticed that David had disappeared. This would have been a good time for her brother to ask his key question about what Todd and Christy wanted to do.

"We've been discussing the options," Todd said calmly. "We haven't come to a conclusion yet."

Christy wished they had. She wished they had every detail planned so that this impromptu meeting would be about their outlining a well-thought-out schedule instead of the free-for-all it was becoming.

As if by prearrangement, footsteps sounded on the front porch, followed by the voices of a couple of Christmas carolers belting out, "We wish you a merry Christmas."

"Do people still do that?" Marti asked.

Christy went to open the door. There stood Rick and Katie, grinning and singing merrily.

"Ho, ho, ho! Wouldn't you know? Your wreath fell off the doe," Katie said, holding out the evergreen circle as Christy invited them to come in.

"It didn't fall off the door. We haven't put it up yet," Christy said. "Todd and I bought it at a tree lot on the way here. I left it on the porch so the pine needles wouldn't get all over the carpet."

"Oh." Katie turned around and returned the wreath to the front porch. "Sorry about that."

"Rick?" Marti called out from the couch. "Rick Doyle? Goodness, we haven't seen you in years."

"I wondered if that was Bob and Marti's Lexus in the driveway," Katie muttered under her breath.

Christy nodded and whispered to Katie, "Your timing is perfect!"

Rick stepped into the living room, where Aunt Marti greeted him with a string of questions.

Marti glanced beyond Christy to see who had come with Rick. "Well, hello, Katie. I suppose you've heard the good news about Todd and Christy."

"No." Katie put on a straight face. "What happened with Todd and Christy? Did they win the lottery?"

"Katie knows." Christy gave Katie a hidden pinch on the arm.

"Ouch!"

"Rick and Katie were both there when I proposed," Todd said.

"Rick, you were there?" Marti's brain seemed to be

working hard to put all the pieces into place. "You didn't tell me all this, Christy."

Rick explained about his position as the manager of The Dove's Nest, and Marti promised she would visit the café sometime.

"Why don't I get us something to eat?" Christy's mom rose from the couch. "You kids must be hungry. Katie, have you and Rick eaten yet?"

"Not exactly," Katie said.

"I'll make some sandwiches."

Christy thought of how some things never changed. Her aunt always would find delight in holding court, and her mother always would revert to feeding people when she didn't know what else to do.

The next hour and a half developed some twists and turns Christy never would have imagined. Todd flipped through one of Marti's bridal magazines in the kitchen while Christy and her mom made sandwiches. Dad went out front and busied himself hanging the wreath. Marti grilled Rick for details of his life since she had last seen him and actually listened respectfully as Rick described his new commitment to Christ and the way his life had changed.

Twice during the conversation Christy exchanged subtle glances with her uncle. Ever since Bob had turned his life over to the Lord, tension had existed between Marti and him since Marti didn't see eye to eye with Bob on his views of Christianity. Over the years Marti had heard it all from Christy and Todd. For some reason she seemed willing to listen to Rick. It was a mystery to Christy.

"We came by to see if you guys want to go Christmas caroling with us tonight," Katie said after they had eaten. "A group is going to meet at the church at six and go from there."

Christy looked at Todd as he rose to help Christy's mom clear the kitchen table. Moving out of the wedding-decision spotlight sounded good to Christy, and the caroling would be fun.

"It's up to you." Todd leaned over and spoke to Christy as he slid past her. "Your aunt and uncle have an hour-and-a-half-drive home. I think they would like a little more information from us before they leave."

Christy excused herself from the table and followed Todd to the kitchen sink, which was less than ten feet away from the company gathered at the table. In a low voice she said, "Are you suggesting we come up with a wedding date right now to satisfy my aunt?"

"Not necessarily."

"I think you and I need to talk about it some more," Christy said. "It needs to be our decision. Yours and mine."

"I agree," Todd said.

"So what do we tell them?"

"That depends. Do you want to go caroling with Rick and Katie?"

"Sure. Do you?"

Todd shrugged. "Whatever."

Just then Christy's mom stepped over to the sink with more dishes. "Are you two going caroling?"

"I guess so," Christy said less than wholeheartedly.

"We don't have to," Todd said quietly.

"I think we should." Christy took a step toward her goal of being more decisive in their relationship. "After all, it is Christmas. We should focus on celebrating Christ's birth, not on figuring out all our wedding plans in one afternoon."

Christy thought her statement made perfect sense. However, later that night, as she and Todd were standing side by side singing "Silent Night," she thought of how her decision—their decision—to go caroling had prompted anything but a silent night around her parents' house. Marti and Bob left with Marti in a controlled huff, and Bob saying, "When you two are ready, you let us know how we can help." David reappeared and announced he had hoped Todd would take him to a movie. Mom returned a stack of board games to the closet after she realized everyone was leaving. And Todd started coughing halfway through the caroling. He stood silently at the last two houses they went to and told Christy his throat was too scratchy to sing.

The ones who seemed to enjoy the caroling the most were Rick and Katie. They were awfully chummy while dashing from house to house, laughing all way— ho, ho, ho.

Bah humbug. I wish we had stayed home where it was warm, even if it meant dealing with my aunt for another few hours. She certainly was ruffled when she left without any answers.

Christy thought about her aunt's comment concerning how long it would take to size a ring. It would take even longer to have one custom made.

We shouldn't be here. Todd and I should be at the mall, checking out the rings at the jewelry stores. Maybe the ring I have in the back of my mind has already been designed, and it's out there somewhere.

One look at Todd told Christy she wouldn't be able to convince this guy to go ring shopping that night. Besides, all the stores probably were closed. They could go tomorrow.

It was almost ten when the caroling concluded. Rick and Katie invited anyone who wanted to join them at Rick's parents' house for his fabulous hot chocolate.

"I'm fried," Todd replied to the invitation. "If you want to go without me, Christy, that's okay."

"No, I'm pretty tired, too."

They strolled back to their car in the church parking lot while the others took off for Rick's house.

"What a night." Christy linked her arm in Todd's and gazed up at the sky. Only a few stars peeked out from behind the thin clouds that looked like lacy ribbons woven through the December sky. "It's so beautiful."

"It is beautiful. And so are you," Todd said in a deep voice. He stopped by the side of their car and drew Christy to him in a warm hug. Pressing his lips against the side of her cheek, he murmured, "So when do you want to get married?"

She could feel his warm breath circling the back of her neck, lacing invisible fingers through her hair. "I don't know. We have to figure it out." She kissed his earlobe. "The sooner the better." She planted a string of little kisses on his neck. "When do you want to get married?"

Todd slowly, deliberately pulled away. "Red light."

"Hmmm?" Christy felt snuggly and dreamy and wanted to stay cuddled up in his warm embrace.

"This is getting a little too, ah . . . yeah. A little too close for me."

A space of several inches now separated them. The cold night air moved right in and sobered Christy.

"I think we're better off talking about this another time. Another place." Todd unlocked Christy's car door. "Until we're married, we're going to be sitting at one very long red light. I don't think it's going to do either of us any good to start revving our engines."

Christy hadn't realized that the close snuggling and her tiny kisses would have such a strong effect on him. "Okay," she agreed, getting into the car. "Red light. I agree."

That moment, as Christy's thoughts cleared in the cold car, she thought, *It's only a few months of sitting at the red light. Then the rest of our lives it will be one long green light. We can wait. We have to wait. We will wait.*

She knew that no matter how many days stretched between that night and their wedding day, what lay ahead were days that would test her heart, mind, and will more than any she had ever experienced.

They didn't talk about their strong feelings on the way home. Todd hummed a song Christy didn't recognize and tapped his fingers on the steering wheel.

Christy thought it would be nice if they could sit in the kitchen and discuss their wedding over their own homemade hot chocolate. But Todd went directly to David's room and crashed on the air mattress Christy's mom had set up for him on the floor.

The next morning Christy showered and dressed and made French toast for breakfast. Her dad had gone to work at his usual 5:30 departure time, and her mom was sleeping in. No sound could be heard from behind the closed door of David's bedroom. At 9:10, on the first Monday of Christmas vacation, Christy sat alone at the kitchen table, eating delicious French toast and reading her Bible. She didn't mind the time alone. It gave her a chance to pray and think. And plan.

She padded on stockinged feet to her bedroom, where she dug into the closet and found a journal-style notebook she never had written in. Returning to the kitchen, she made herself a cup of tea and christened the journal her wedding planner. On the cover page she wrote *Todd and Christy* in loopy letters and then playfully drew a big heart around their names. Turning to the first page, Christy listed every detail she could think of that needed to be discussed. She was three pages into the list when Mom joined her in the kitchen.

"I thought you might have slept in," Mom said. "The boys are still asleep."

"I have too much on my mind. I made lots of French toast. It's in the microwave, if you want to warm it up and have some."

"What a treat! Thank you."

Before Christy's mom could join her at the table, Christy heard the bedroom door open down the hall. A minute later she heard the shower turn on in the bathroom. Ten minutes later, Todd emerged, blowing his nose.

"Oh, sorry," he said when he noticed Christy and her mom. "I didn't realize you were there. I thought a shower might help my sinuses but . . ." He began to cough.

"Sounds like you have the flu." Mom stepped over to feel Todd's forehead. "Oh dear, you're burning up. Is your throat sore?"

Todd nodded.

"Why don't you go back to bed? I'll bring you some hot tea."

"I can get it for him, Mom." Christy hopped up. "Do you want to try eating anything?"

"No, a little juice is all I want. I should get on the road and head back to my dad's house."

"Even though you're sick?" Mom asked.

"Why would you go to your dad's?" Christy asked.

Todd leaned against the kitchen counter. "I told him I'd be home today so we could spend some time together. He has this week off work."

"I didn't know that. I thought you were planning to stay here all week." Christy looked at her long list and thought of all the items she had planned to start checking off in the next few days.

"Why don't you stay here until you're better?" Mom asked. "It won't do your dad any good to have you bring home a flu bug with you."

"I don't think it's going to do your family any good if I stay." Todd turned his head and covered his mouth as he coughed some more.

"You sound awful." Christy felt bad that she had put her to-do list ahead of her fiancé's health. "Why don't you go back to bed? At least for a few hours."

Todd nodded. "I'll lie down for an hour. I'm guessing the fever will be gone by then."

"I'll get you some juice," Christy said. A few minutes later she carried in some cranberry juice on a tray, along with a thermometer, a box of tissues, a cold washcloth, a box of cold and flu tablets, and some cough drops.

Todd didn't want any of it. Not even the juice.

"Just water," he said with his eyes closed. He had bundled himself up and was lying there with the hood of his navy blue sweat shirt pulled over his head, looking as if he was determined to sweat out every drop of flu virus.

When Christy returned with the water, he took only a sip and rolled over. David was up and dressed, so Todd had the room to himself. He stayed there in a deep hibernation, occasionally punctuated by a raspy cough, for the entire day.

At dinnertime he came out of his cave and announced he was driving home. This time he had all four members of the Miller family to argue with.

"Just sleep," Mom urged.

"Get some fluids in you," Christy pleaded.

"Take another shower," David suggested.

Christy had to agree; Todd didn't smell his freshest. He looked awful.

"Let me wash your sweat shirt," Mom said. "Do you have anything clean to put on after your shower?"

Todd looked irritated. "I'm okay. I can take it from here. Thanks for letting me sleep."

Christy realized that Todd, an only child who lived with his divorced dad since he was young, probably never had anyone to baby him when he was sick. After his car accident, he was willing to let others care for him, but that was different. In matters of the flu, Todd seemed to prefer to go it alone.

Despite another round of protests, Todd carried his stuff out to the car at a little after seven that evening. Christy followed him to the driveway. As Todd climbed into their car, he said, "I'll see you at Bob and Marti's on Christmas Eve."

Christy didn't mean to let her thoughts slip out, but before she could stop them, the words "What about getting a ring?" tumbled from her mouth. She realized how selfish and inconsiderate it sounded, but it was too late.

"I heard you say last night you were planning to go to the mall with your mom this week." Todd fastened his seat belt. "Why don't you look for rings while you're with her?"

The thought of shopping for an engagement ring with her mother didn't sit right with Christy. "I'll wait until you and I can go shopping."

"You're not shopping; you're just looking. I thought you were pretty close to figuring out what you wanted."

"Yes, but—"

"Listen." Todd covered his mouth and coughed something awful. "I want you to end up with a ring you really like. I'm guessing it's going to take you a little while to make your final decision. I don't think you need me to look at everything with you."

Christy recognized he was trying to be understanding and patient. She felt terrible for even bringing up the topic.

"Don't worry about it," Christy said. "You just work on getting better. We can talk on Christmas Eve."

"Okay. Thanks, honey. I appreciate your understanding."

Christy didn't remember him ever calling her "honey" before, and she thought it was awfully sweet. She also thought of how 1 Corinthians 13 described true love as "patient." That took on deeper meaning for her now as she realized she would have to place the ring hunt on hold. Todd had told her their future together would be full of adjustments. She didn't like having to adjust, but it seemed she had no choice.

Todd reached for her hand, but instead of kissing her good-bye, he held her hand and gave her three squeezes. With each squeeze he said, "I-love-you."

Christy gave him three squeezes back and repeated the message, "I-love-you. I'll see you Thursday. Please take care of yourself."

"I always have." Todd slowly backed out of the driveway.

Christy watched their blue Volvo cruise quietly down the street. Inside, she missed him already.

Am I going to feel this way for the rest of my life? Every time he leaves, am I going to feel like a part of me has gone with him?

"Father, please send your guardian angels to watch over my Todd as he drives to his dad's tonight. Keep him safe. And, Lord, even though he thinks he's always taken care of himself, I know that you have been the One who has really watched over him. Please take care of him tonight."

Todd stopped at the corner and honked the horn three times. Christy smiled. "Yeah, I love you, too, ya big lug."

By Tuesday evening of Christmas vacation, Christy had a good idea of what she wanted her ring to look like. She had made a rough sketch in her wedding notebook and pasted three magazine photos of rings on the same page. She and her mom had gone to the mall that morning and looked in several jewelry stores. They also had thumbed through a book of invitations in a stationery store, discussed the color of the bridesmaids' dresses over frozen yogurt, and picked up information on the cost of tux rentals.

Christy had spent an hour on the phone with Todd before dinner telling him all the details.

"You sound good," Todd said in a raspy voice.

"You sound awful," Christy countered.

"I know. This cold is really hanging on. What I meant is that you sound happy. I'm glad you and your mom got to spend some time together and work on a few of the details."

Christy couldn't resist teasing Todd. "You're just

saying that because you're happy you weren't the one being dragged through the mall today."

"Yeah, I am," Todd said.

"Are you sure you didn't fake that cold to get out of spending the week here planning with me?"

"Nothing is fake about this beast," Todd said. "I don't remember the last time I felt this awful."

"Maybe you should go to the doctor," Christy suggested. "You might have strep throat. Didn't you say your ears hurt? If the virus settles in your ears, you could have an ear infection, and you'll need antibiotics to clear it up."

"That's okay, Christy. I'm sure I'll be all right in a few days." Todd's voice carried a hint of aggravation. Christy realized she was being motherly, and that was something Todd never had responded well to.

"Sorry," she said. "I hope you feel better."

"I will. I'll be over this by the time you see me Thursday."

Todd's prediction turned out to be wishful thinking.

When Christy and her family arrived at Bob and Marti's house, Todd took Christy in his arms and held her close. "I missed you so much." His voice was little more than a gravelly whisper.

"I missed you, too."

They stood in the kitchen, holding each other, slightly swaying, neither of them willing to let go.

"I love you." She leaned close and brushed his cheek with a kiss.

"Aw, come on, you guys. Cut it out." David had stepped into the kitchen with his sleeping bag and suitcase and made an exaggerated effort to walk around them. "You guys are making a spectacle of yourselves."

"A spectacle?" Todd repeated in a hoarse whisper, followed by a horrible-sounding laugh.

Christy laughed at her brother as well as at Todd's laryngitis-affected laughter.

"I'm impressed, David. When did you start using words like 'spectacle'?" Todd asked.

"What happened to your voice?" David replied.

Todd shrugged and gave a sheepish grin, as if he had misplaced his voice and wasn't sure where he had put it.

"Are you still sick?" David asked.

"I feel a lot better," Todd said.

"Dad wants you guys to help carry in the presents," David said.

Christy slipped her hand into Todd's, and he squeezed three times. She smiled and returned the squeezes. They walked out to the driveway hand in hand, smiling.

Aunt Marti stood beside the car and viewed them skeptically. "I hope you didn't kiss her, Todd. The last thing Christy needs is to get sick. It's a wonder all of us didn't end up with the flu since we were with you on Sunday."

"If I had known I was getting sick, I wouldn't have gone over to the Millers and exposed everyone."

Todd's pathetically thin voice added to the apologetic expression on his face.

Marti seemed satisfied with his response. She waited while Christy's dad loaded the two of them up with gear from the car. Then she picked up the handles of a shopping bag full of Christmas gifts and followed Todd and Christy into the kitchen.

"I have a few things to go over with you two right away."

"Like what?" Christy asked cautiously.

"Oh, just a few items we need to discuss. I thought we could sit down and go over all this now." Marti planted the handled bag on the kitchen floor and pointed to the oak table in the kitchen's corner.

Christy noticed several stacks of paper neatly stapled together and placed in front of the chairs as if in preparation for a business meeting.

"I think we should help my dad unload the car first," Christy said.

"I'll make some coffee," Marti said. "As soon as you're finished, please join me."

"Where's Uncle Bob?" Christy instinctively knew it would be a good idea to have her uncle nearby when Marti started in on the two of them.

"He went to pick up our Christmas Eve dinner. We ordered everything from D'Angelo's this year. Bob is going to prepare it for us, and we'll eat at six. That gives us a little more than an hour for our meeting. I mean, our discussion."

Christy's dad entered with his arms full, and Mom was right behind him.

"Does anything else need to come in?" Todd asked.

"No, this is the last of it," Dad said. "Would someone move this bag of gifts so I don't knock it over?"

Christy quickly scooped up the handled bag Marti had left in the middle of the floor. Carrying it into the living room, she placed each of the gifts under the tree. Bob and Marti had set up the Christmas tree in its usual spot in front of their beach-front home's huge window. Marti went all out decorating and changed her theme every year. This year the tree was a Douglas fir that touched the ceiling and filled the living room with a fresh, outdoor fragrance. Marti had chosen to decorate with just two colors, white and red. She even had changed the window treatment to white velvet swags across the top, held in place with wide red velvet bows.

Tiny white lights, looking like icicles, hung from the ceiling. More tiny lights glimmered from every branch on the tree. All the ornaments were red. Christy examined a tiny red sled that hung from one of the branches. Beside it was a red apple ornament tied to the tree with a red-and-white-plaid ribbon.

Christy was about to return to the kitchen when she noticed an envelope attached to a red-striped ribbon that looped over one of the lower branches. The envelope had David's name on it, but for some reason, the sight of it reminded her of Rick's envelope.

I never did open that envelope. I wonder where I put it?

"Christina," Marti called from the kitchen, "the coffee is ready."

Christy drew in a deep breath and headed for the kitchen. Todd, her parents, and Marti were all seated, waiting for her.

As soon as Christy slid her chair close to Todd's, Marti dived in. "I should begin by telling you I took the liberty of calling my country club this week and found that they miraculously had a cancellation the last weekend of June. Of course, I reserved it. I had to put down a substantial deposit, but as you might guess, the only other opening was at the end of November and—"

"Wait," Christy said. "Open for what? What are you talking about?"

Marti pointed to the first item of business on the printed agenda that rested on the top of the papers stacked in front of each seat. "The reservation for your wedding. I can't think of a nicer place to have your ceremony than at the Newport Country Club, can you?"

Christy shot a stunned look at her mother, who was sitting directly across from her.

Her mother said, "Your father and I were under the impression you would get married at our church in Escondido. We could hold the reception in the gym. They have lots of round tables that we could cover with—"

"A gymnasium!" Marti looked at her sister incredulously. "You can't be serious, Margaret. You wouldn't want your only daughter to have her reception in a gymnasium!"

"Our church has receptions in the gym all the time. I went to a luncheon there last spring that was lovely. They hung ferns from the basketball backboards and—"

"I won't hear of it," Marti said firmly. "Christy deserves an elegant, classy wedding. She and Todd should have the best facility available for the most memorable day of their lives. Don't you understand it was a minor miracle for me to secure the Newport Beach Country Club in June?"

Marti turned to Christy and Todd with a pleading expression. "I thought you two, of all people, would see this as a sign from God that you should get married the last Saturday in June."

A dead-air moment followed. Christy didn't know where to begin in her argument with her aunt. Her mother appeared mortally wounded, and her father was looking down into his coffee cup.

Todd leaned back and broke the tension by saying in his raspy whisper, "I'm confident the Bridegroom will show up wherever we hold the ceremony."

Marti's expression showed she didn't appreciate his comment. "Of course you will show up, Todd. That's not the point."

"I didn't mean me. I meant *the* Bridegroom. Jesus Christ. He's with us here right now. He'll show up wherever Christy and I are on the day that we promise our lives to each other. That's all that really matters."

Marti's face grew red. "Todd, I have held my tongue for a very long time, but I can't remain silent any longer." She leaned across the table and with fire in her eyes said, "I love you like a son. You know that. There is nothing I wouldn't do for you or give you. But you have failed to show me the slightest courtesy in areas that matter the most to me. I've listened to you spiritualize for the last time."

She rose to her feet and pressed white knuckles to the table. "This is not about your heavenly view of everything. This is the wedding day of my one and only niece. I am offering my time and my resources to help create an unforgettable day for the two of you. And how do you respond? By being rude, disrespectful, and inconsiderate. Well, that's it!"

Todd stood. "You're right." His voice broke, and he reverted to a loud whisper. "I haven't honored your considerable efforts. I'm sorry. Will you forgive me for being insensitive and not appreciating all you do for Christy and me?"

Marti didn't seem to know how to respond. She stood rigidly and stared at Todd as if trying to determine if he was sincere or if this was another spiritual tactic to break down her defenses.

Todd waited. His expression was open and expectant.

Marti continued to stare at him; her jaw remained firm.

"Ho! Ho! Ho!" came a jovial voice as the door to the garage opened. "It's Santa and his helper! Have we got a prime rib dinner for you! And wait until you see the cheesecake . . ." Bob stopped in his tracks and sized up the standoff at the kitchen table.

"What happened?" David asked, following Uncle Bob and carrying a large white cake box.

Marti tilted her head slightly and in a low voice said, "I suggest we start over. Let's all take a deep breath and go on from here."

"That won't erase the offense." Todd cleared his throat and tried to continue. "I hurt you, Marti. I was wrong. I apologize. Please forgive me."

With a wave of her hand and a stilted laugh, Marti said, "Don't worry about it, Todd. We're all running on heightened emotions. I suggest we take a five-minute break and then reconvene with an agreement to all communicate with a renewed level of respect."

Christy thought her aunt had turned into a robot and was spouting phrases she had heard before rather than saying what sprang from her heart. Maybe that was how issues were discussed when Marti was involved with the art colony.

"What did we miss?" David asked.

Mom shot him a look that said, "Don't ask such questions, David!"

"Are we still on for a six-o'clock dinner?" Bob asked, unloading his bags of food on the counter. "Or should we adjust that?"

"Six-thirty would be better." Marti moved over to the coffee maker and poured a fresh cup of coffee. "We're just getting started."

Uncle Bob caught Christy's eye. He held her gaze with a silent, questioning look. Christy gave a little nod and mouthed the words, "It's okay."

Bob slowly nodded.

"Would it be all right if I made some tea?" Christy asked.

"Of course," Bob said. "You know where it is. Help yourself. I bought some Christmas peppermint tea yesterday that you might like. How about you, Todd? A little something warm for your throat? Or would cold feel better? We have plenty of everything."

"Tea."

"I'll get it." Christy rubbed Todd's back as she slid past him. "Is peppermint okay?"

He nodded.

Christy had just turned on the flame under the teakettle when Marti returned to the table and announced they were ready to continue.

"Go ahead and sit down," Bob suggested to Christy. "I'll bring your tea over to you."

With fresh determination, Marti went back to her agenda, skipping the first point until later. "Let's go on to the third point. The cake. If you will look at the third and fourth pages on your handout, you will see some color copies that are examples of Cakes by Emilie. Her bakery is in great demand because she interviews the couples, finds out what is meaningful to them, and then designs a cake specifically for them. No two cakes are ever alike."

"Are those skateboards on the border of that yellow

cake?" Christy's mom asked.

"Cool!" David looked over Christy's shoulder. "How did they make the little black wheels? Is that a birthday cake?"

"No, these are all wedding cakes. The groom was an architect. He met his bride when he was designing a skate park for the city of Solana Beach. I asked about that one because I thought it was unusual, too."

Christy wanted to protest the use of skateboards as an appropriate decoration on a wedding cake so Todd wouldn't get any ideas about using surfboards on theirs. But she knew it would be better not to challenge her aunt. At least not yet.

Marti seemed to have calmed down. David went into the den to watch TV, and Bob brought Christy and Todd their tea and then quietly worked in the kitchen while Marti worked her way down the list. She went on with her presentation for fifteen uninterrupted minutes. No one else said a word. No one agreed or disagreed or challenged her on any of her seven points. When she returned to the first two points, she presented her opinions with an enthusiastic tone.

"As I mentioned earlier, I went ahead and reserved the country club for June. Point number two is the wedding coordinator I've been working with to gather all this information. Her name is Elise, and I made an appointment for us to meet with her on Saturday afternoon at two o'clock. Now for discussion. Who has questions?"

No one moved or spoke up.

Christy had so many conflicting feelings she didn't dare try to say anything. Todd was the brave one again. For a man with so little voice left, he was sure set on having his say. "Thank you, Marti. You worked hard on all this. I appreciate it. This will help Christy and me as we make our decisions and put everything together."

Christy thought his choice of words was great. "Put everything together" could mean they would take all Aunt Marti's ideas, some of her ideas, or none of her ideas. The part Marti heard was the thank-you. That seemed more important than anything else.

"You're welcome. This is only the beginning, you know. We have much more planning to do. That's where Elise will help us out on Saturday."

Christy determined right then and there that she and Todd would find time in the next day and a half to talk through all their wedding plans. They would decide on their own, just the two of them, when, where, and how they would get married. If they had to stay up all night for the next two nights, they would form their own plan. If they had to go somewhere else to talk, they wouldn't come back until they had their own completed list. Even if Todd lost his voice completely and could only communicate by sign language, they *would* figure out everything before two o'clock on Saturday. And the decisions would be all theirs because, after all, this was their wedding.

CHRISTY AND TODD
THE COLLEGE YEARS

7 "Wait a minute," Katie said, stopping in the middle of the produce section at the grocery store. "Todd and you went ahead and met with the wedding coordinator on Saturday even though you guys don't want to get married at the yacht club?"

It was the Monday after Christmas, and Katie and Christy had returned to Rancho Corona to prepare for the Mexico outreach trip with Todd's youth group. Christy and Katie hadn't seen each other since the night they went caroling but had agreed earlier on the phone to meet in front of the grocery store down the hill from their college campus.

They stood in the parking lot talking for nearly ten minutes before Christy suggested they shop while they talked. Entering the grocery store with Katie pushing the cart, Christy continued to summarize her Christmas weekend at Bob and Marti's in a more positive tone than she felt.

"Yes, we met with the wedding coordinator,"

Christy said. "She's not from the club. She's independent. I liked her. She had a lot of good ideas for us."

"So when did you tell your aunt that you don't want to have the ceremony at the yacht club?"

"We haven't told her yet, but we will," Christy said. "Todd and I spent hours discussing everything even though his voice was barely above a whisper."

"And after all your discussing you didn't come up with a wedding date?"

"We have a possible date." Christy checked her shopping list and put a bag of red apples into the cart.

"As your best friend and possible maid of honor, may I ask what your possible wedding date is? Or are you keeping it a secret from everyone?"

"It's not a secret, Katie. The date is May twenty-second. But you're the only one who knows it so don't say anything until we can confirm it. And you are more than my possible maid of honor. You *are* my maid of honor. Or I should say, I'd like you to be, if you want to."

"Of course. I'm honored. Honored to be your maid of honor. But now I have to ask, how did you come up with May twenty-second as your date? I thought Todd wanted to get married sooner."

"Todd and I went over every possible weekend between now and next Christmas. Believe me, the only date that worked was May twenty-second. We wanted to have at least a week for our honeymoon, and that was the only time we could fit it in. It's nine days after I graduate and nine days before Todd starts to work full time at the church for the summer."

"Okay, that makes sense," Katie said. "But I still don't get it. Why didn't you announce you had decided on a date?"

"Because we don't know if we can have the meadow yet. We have to wait until the Rancho Corona administration people return to their offices next week."

"Wait a minute. I am so lost. What meadow?" Katie had stopped pushing the cart and looked as if she wasn't going to move until Christy explained every detail.

"The meadow at school. By the chapel. That's where we want to hold the ceremony and the reception."

"You're kidding."

"No, that's where we want to get married."

Katie tilted her head and scrutinized Christy. "How do your parents feel about that? I would think they would want you to have the ceremony at their church in Escondido."

"They do."

"But you don't."

"We want to get married in the meadow." Christy pulled the cart over toward the bread and tossed in five of the least-expensive loaves.

"Could you change one of those whole wheat loaves to white?" Katie asked. "Rick likes white bread. His mom made these incredible leftover turkey sandwiches on white bread the day after Christmas. Have you ever had a turkey sandwich with stuffing and cranberry sauce?"

Now Christy was the one tilting her head and scrutinizing Katie. "No, it sounds good."

"It's my new favorite. But it has to be on white bread. The stuffing makes it all stick together." Katie pushed the cart toward the peanut butter and jelly. "Didn't you have peanut butter on the list? I think the cheapest jelly is this big bucket of grape."

Christy told Katie to pick up three jars of peanut butter and then said, "So tell me all about your Christmas. How did everything go with Rick?"

"Great. Wonderful." Katie put the peanut butter in the cart. "But you didn't finish telling me about you and Todd. Is he going to be well enough to go to Mexico?"

"Yes, he's fine now. His voice is almost back to normal. There's not much else to tell about our plans. We didn't get to the jewelers so we don't have a ring yet. And I already told you we have to check on reserving the meadow before we can set our date."

"And break the shocking news to your aunt and everyone else."

"Exactly," Christy said. "Oh, and my uncle offered us the use of his condo on Maui for our honeymoon."

Katie grinned. "Well, at least you have one important detail taken care of."

Christy motioned for Katie to push the grocery cart down the canned-food aisle. She studied the prices on the tomato sauce cans.

"You know," Katie said, "if you get married in the meadow, you can release butterflies instead of the usual."

Christy laughed at her friend's suggestion. "Don't you dare suggest that one to my aunt! She already has a long list of creative ideas for our cake and my veil and the bouquet."

"I'm serious," Katie said. "I saw it on TV. The bride ordered these butterflies that came in individual boxes. They looked like Chinese takeout boxes. As soon as the couple said 'I do,' the guests opened the boxes. I thought it was a great idea."

"Well, we're not going to say 'I do.' "

"You're not?"

"We talked about our vows last night. Todd and I decided we're going to say 'I promise,' because that makes it clearer that we're making a vow to love, honor, and cherish and all the rest of it."

"I'm sure the butterflies would flap their little wings on cue whether you said 'I do' or 'I promise,' " Katie said sarcastically. "Or if you want to hold the butterflies until the end, you can launch butterflies at the same time you heave your bouquet."

Katie's expression created an image in Christy's mind of "launched" butterflies and "heaved" flowers all tumbling through the air in the meadow.

"Now tell me, Katie." Christy faced her friend. "Would I be making an accurate guess if I said I should plan to heave my bouquet in your direction?"

"You can heave it anywhere you want," Katie said.

" 'The Lord will fulfill his purpose for me.' "

Christy raised her eyebrows, trying to interpret Katie's response.

"That's my new verse. Rick and I found it this weekend. It's in Psalm 138. Verse 8. Took us only two seconds to memorize it. 'The Lord will fulfill his purpose for me.' That's it. Isn't that incredible? I've decided to make that my life verse. How many cans of spaghetti sauce did you want?"

Christy checked her list. "Six of those large ones on the lower shelf. Get the brand on the right; it's four cents less."

"Do you want these jumbo-sized packages of spaghetti noodles?"

"Yes, three of those, and why don't you grab one more can of sauce just to be sure we have enough."

"That's right," Katie said. "Doug is coming. He eats more than anyone I know. Tracy is still planning to come, isn't she?"

"The last I heard she was."

"I hope she's not having a lot of morning sickness," Katie said. "That wouldn't be much fun in Mexico."

"Maybe she won't be able to come after all," Christy said. "I'll give her a call tonight. Do you have any gum or mints with you? My throat is really dry."

"No. Do you want me to get some gum at the checkout for you?"

"No, I'll buy some cough drops when we go down that aisle. It would be good to have some with us in Mexico. I already put together a first-aid kit, but I didn't add any cough drops."

"I wish Sierra and the rest of her gang would have come back early from Christmas break so they could join us," Katie said.

"We might make another trip in the spring. From what Todd said, this orphanage needs a lot of work."

"Rick might have to leave early. Did I tell you that? He's having a hard time with the work schedule for the end of the week. I might come back with him, unless you still need my help with the food and everything."

"It's only for four days," Christy said. "I mean, if you have to leave early, that's okay. But it's not a very long trip."

"I know. And he might be able to work it out so he can stay the whole time. The problem with being the manager of The Dove's Nest is that he's the one who's ultimately responsible, you know? They really need more help on weekdays."

"Are you still planning to work there?" Christy asked.

"Yes. I start right after New Year's. I might as well have started last week because I was in every day Rick was there. I've already pretty much learned everything I need to know to start taking orders. I have a feeling I'm really going to like working there."

Christy bit her lip. She had almost said, "Oh, and I wonder why?" But she didn't want to jeopardize her communication with Katie. Especially after the tangle they had had more than a week ago in their dorm room.

The rest of their shopping went smoothly. Unfortunately, Katie didn't open up much about her budding relationship with Rick.

After they unloaded all the groceries at the church kitchen, picked up a pizza, and returned to their dorm room, Christy was hopeful Katie would open up more. However, a minor distraction consumed their attention.

Katie unlocked their dorm room door with the pizza box in her hand and immediately froze in place.

Christy didn't have to ask what made Katie stop and stare. Christy already knew. Todd had come with her to the dorm room earlier that morning and had carried in the object Katie now was gaping at.

"It's my Christmas present from Todd," Christy said in a low voice. "He made it."

"Ohhh! Is that Naranja?" Katie slowly stepped into the room, sounding as if she were recognizing a long-lost friend.

"Yes, the backrest is Todd's old surfboard, Naranja. And that's the backseat from Gus the bus. Todd sort of welded them together and now . . . it's . . . a couch, I guess."

"What do you mean it's a couch, you guess?" Katie sat down and looked up at Christy with an expression of delight. "This is the most amazing, authentic, memory-filled *objet d'art* I've ever seen. I could just cry! And you know what? It's actually sort of comfy, too."

Christy forced a smile. It was the same smile she had forced when Todd presented her with his unique gift on Christmas. He had tied a long red string to the homemade sofa and hid it in the garage at Bob and Marti's. He looped the string all the way through the house, and Christy was full of giggles and anticipation as she followed the thread. But when she opened the garage door and saw the one-of-a-kind couch sitting there with a big red bow on it, she was speechless.

Todd, on the other hand, raspy voice and all, couldn't stop talking about his creation. He had gotten the idea while recovering from the car accident and had worked on it for several weeks at his dad's before coming up with the right combination of parts to hold the surfboard in place as the backrest to the car's bench seat. He was so proud of himself that Christy knew she had to offer some kind of praise.

After the oohing and ahhing event was over, Christy felt she should have been nominated for an Oscar in the category of best supporting actress in a romantic comedy.

"Don't you love it?" Katie adjusted her position and stretched out her legs. Then, as if in need of an appropriate prop, she reached into the carryout box and grabbed a slice of pizza.

Christy delivered one of her well-rehearsed lines. "I appreciate Todd's hard work. It's very creative."

Katie stopped munching. "You hate it, don't you? Did you tell him that?"

Christy reached for a slice of pizza, and with a sigh she flopped on the edge of her bed. "No, of course not. It would have devastated him."

With quiet bites, Katie adjusted her position again. "Does Todd consider this actual furniture?"

Christy nodded. "We have a couch and a camp stove. Todd thinks all we need now are two sleeping bags that zip together, and we can start our life of marital bliss."

Katie cracked up. "I'm sorry. That's not funny, is it? Does Todd have any idea how clueless he is when it comes to civilization stuff? I mean, he's a great guy, but his idea of normal life is . . . well . . . you would think he had spent his life in a jungle hut."

"In some ways, I think he did," Christy said. "Not a jungle hut, of course. Although, I'm sure he would have enjoyed that. I think his growing up as an only child and living with his dad made him a minimalist. The more we discuss our plans for the future, the more obvious our differences become."

"And you are telling him what's important to you as you go along, aren't you?" Katie asked.

Christy thought hard before nodding her head. "Yes, most of the time."

Katie put down her half-eaten piece of pizza and walked over to where Christy sat on her bed. With Katie's face mere inches from Christy's, she shouted, "Hello! This is your wake-up call!"

Christy turned away. She found her friend's tactics annoying and unhelpful.

Katie returned to the surfboard sofa and resumed her pizza consumption with a critical eye fixed on Christy. "That was a little too overt, wasn't it? Sorry.

But you get my point, don't you?"

"Yes, I get your point, Katie."

"I mean, you guys are marrying each other. This is getting serious. This *is* serious. Let me ask you one thing. Do you want to get married in the meadow or was that Todd's idea?"

"It was Todd's idea, but I like it."

"Are you sure?"

Christy nodded.

"Are you falling into one of those zombie modes where you don't know what you want and you don't care?"

"I care!"

"Don't get upset," Katie said. "I'm just looking at you, and you're looking kind of spacey."

"I'm fine. I'm a little tired, but that's all. Todd and I need to work on our communication skills," Christy said. "And we are. We will. Todd is going to talk to one of the pastors at church about setting up some pre-marital counseling sessions for us. I think that will help."

Katie nodded.

"It's not like we aren't communicating at all," Christy said defensively. "It's just that we both want to get better at it. All couples have to make a lot of adjustments. We'll work it out."

In a calm voice Katie said, "I know you will."

They were quiet for a minute. Christy felt her head pounding. She had been trying to ignore a growing headache since they were grocery shopping, but now it was on her with full force.

"That saying about opposites attracting must be true," Katie said. "You and Todd are opposite in a lot of ways. Maybe that indicates you'll balance each other out."

"That's what Todd says," Christy said. "He's says we're good for each other because we think differently and do things differently."

"Hmm." Katie reached for a second slice of pizza.

"What are you *hmm*ing about?"

Katie picked a slice of pepperoni off her pizza, and a long string of mozzarella cheese followed the pepperoni up to her mouth. "Do you think Rick and I are opposites?"

Christy paused only a moment before saying with a sly grin, "Oh, did you just notice that?"

"That could be a good thing, couldn't it?" Katie cast a sideways glance at Christy, as if her future might be determined by the way Christy responded to this all-important question.

"Yes, it could be a good thing," Christy said. "It could be a God-thing for all I know."

Katie nodded thoughtfully. "Yes, it could. It could be a really surprising God-thing. Hmm. Who would have guessed?"

"Not me," Christy said quietly.

Christy hoped Katie would take that as an opportunity to open up about what was going on with Rick. But Katie announced she had to get going. Grabbing another piece of pizza, she bounced up and left to meet Rick at The Dove's Nest before Christy had even finished her first slice of pizza.

Alone in her dorm room, Christy stared at the surfboard sofa. It took up the center open area of their room. "You belong in a store that sells wet suits and skateboards," she muttered to the bright orange fiberglass room centerpiece. "Not here. What was Todd thinking?"

Once again she reminded herself Todd had lovingly taken two of the only valuable items he had owned in his life and had tried to salvage them and make them into something useful. That was commendable. It was sweet of him to give it to Christy. She needed to be more appreciative.

Why can't I be spontaneous and enthusiastic about things like Katie? Why can't I let whatever comes just come?

She glanced at the alarm clock and realized it was almost time for her to pick up Todd at church. He had promised her they would go ring shopping that evening. The plan was for them to stay at her parents' house that night. In the morning they would drive back to church and start the huge task of packing up all the gear for the Mexico trip.

However, by the time Christy had gathered her things and had met Todd at church, she was feeling awful.

"Do you have a fever?" Todd asked when they were about ten minutes from her parents' house.

"I don't think so. I feel kind of cold. I have a ripping headache."

Todd reached over and felt her forehead. "You have a fever. At least it started here and not in Mexico. You'll feel better by Friday, and you'll sound better by the time classes start up again a week from today."

"What makes you so sure I have the same virus you had?"

"It's going around. If you didn't catch it from me, you probably got it from that wedding coordinator on Saturday. Do you remember how she said her throat felt scratchy? That's how it starts."

Christy swallowed. Now her throat hurt. "I can't get sick. I have to do the food in Mexico."

"I can do it. Or Doug or Rick and Katie. Tracy isn't coming because of her morning sickness."

"I might feel better in the morning," Christy said. "We don't have to go ring shopping tonight. I could head right to bed when we get to my parents' house. That will help a lot, I'm sure."

Todd wore a knowing grin as he pulled into her parents' driveway. "I'll bring in your stuff. Why don't you go on in. I'll see you in a week."

Christy shot Todd an incredulous look. "What do you mean you'll see me in a week? I'll get some good sleep and be ready to go in the morning. You'll see."

Todd broke into a full smile as he turned off the engine. "Yes, dear. Whatever you say."

Todd was right. Christy was sick for a week.

8 His being right bugged her for the first three days she lay in bed feeling miserable. She was missing the Mexico trip and missing Todd and missing the latest developments with Rick and Katie.

The only thing she wasn't missing was the wastebasket. After going through two boxes of tissues, she had become an expert at tossing the tissue into the wicker wastebasket in the corner.

Christy had made an observation about another difference between Todd and her. When she was sick, she wanted lots of attention every hour on the hour. She didn't care for the caveman approach to "sweating it out" and cutting oneself off from all forms of society until the virus had run its course.

By day three, Thursday, Christy was convinced the highlight of the week had been her mother's kind attention, which came complete with daily doses of toast and herbal tea sweetened with honey. The most depressing part of her confinement had been realizing how different things were going to be once she and Todd were married. Her mother would no longer bring toast and tea and put fresh sheets on the bed while Christy soaked in the tub. She conjured up a disturbing image of herself lying in a contorted position on the surfboard sofa while trying to lean over and light the camp stove to heat water for her already used tea bag.

I have to tell him, that's all. I have to tell Todd what I want and what I need. When we're married, if he knows that I want him to bring me tea, I'm sure he'll gladly do that. I just have to tell him.

An idea occurred to Christy that afternoon. She was over the achy fever part of the flu and into the laryngitis phase. She was feeling well enough to get up, but she decided to spend one more day in bed just to be sure.

With her bedroom door closed, Christy pulled out from under her bed a shoe box she had covered with wrapping paper years ago. Inside the shoe box were fourteen letters, all sealed in individual envelopes. On the cover of each envelope she had written the same four words, *To my future husband.*

A satisfying smile started in the secret corner of Christy's heart and, like sweet-smelling perfume, wafted its way to Christy's lips. When she had started writing those letters, she didn't know whom she would marry. Many times she had hoped it would be Todd, but every time she had deposited another letter into the box, she hadn't been sure the letter would end up in Todd's hands.

Today she knew. Todd was the man she had saved herself for. He would be the one to read those letters on their wedding night. He would know even more fully that for the past five years she had prayed for him, waited for him, hoped in him.

Christy decided she had one more letter to write. Pulling a piece of stationery out of a box she had purchased in Switzerland, Christy began the letter with,

Dear Future Husband, my Todd,

It felt good to write his name in the greeting. He didn't have a middle name, which Christy thought was unfortunate. Their children would all have middle names. Noble, poetic-sounding middle names like hers, which was Juliet.

Proceeding with the letter, she wrote,

As I write this, you're in Mexico, and I'm in bed with the flu. I've had some time to think these past few days, and I want to tell you two things. No, three. First, I'm so happy we're getting married. I can't wait to be your wife. I know we'll have a lot of adjusting to do, but we'll work on it together. I know we'll become better communicators.

And that brings me to my second thought. Whenever I'm sick, I need attention. I don't like to be left alone to sweat it out. I'd like you to check on me and bring me tea and toast. I know we're different in this area, and I thought you should know this is important to me.

I remember one time in high school when I was sick, and you came to my parents' house and sat by my bed doing

your homework while I slept. Maybe you thought that once I woke up I'd spring out of bed, and we could go do something. But you were there with me. I never told you that I considered that one of the most romantic and tender memories of our early years together. I can't wait until we're married so that every morning when I wake up the first thing I'll see is your handsome face. Soon.

Now, on to my final thought before I get lost in a daydream about our future together. I want all our children to have middle names, okay?

With all my love, forever,
Your Christina Juliet Miller
(soon to be Spencer)!

P.S. I love you.

Sealing the letter in an envelope, Christy wrote on the front, *To my Todd.*

She tucked away the letter with the others and returned the box to its hiding place under her bed. The letter reminded her of something: Rick's letter.

Where did I put Rick's letter?

A tap sounded on her bedroom door, and her mom entered. "How are you feeling?"

"I'm feeling lots better." As soon as she spoke, she started a coughing jag that made her sound anything but better.

"I thought I heard you moving around in here. Would you like me to bring you anything?"

"Did Marti leave those bridal magazines here?"

Mom nodded. "They're in the living room. Would you like me to get them?"

"Please."

For the rest of the afternoon, Christy browsed through the magazines. As darkness came over the world outside her window, she slumped into a nap in which she dreamed of a fashion show of outrageous bridal dresses punctuated by advertisements for Oneida silverware.

By one o'clock the next afternoon, Christy had cut several dozen pictures from the assortment of bridal magazines and pasted them into her wedding planner notebook. She felt as if she were playing paper dolls as she cut the bodice from one gown and matched it with the skirt from another. She found the exact dress she wanted for the bridesmaids. It was shown in an apricot color, but she wanted it in pale blue. Four different veils looked as though they might work for her, but she decided it would be difficult to know unless she tried them on.

Putting away her notebook and pulling out a pair of jeans and a sweat shirt from the stack of clean clothes her mom had washed and folded, Christy headed for the shower. She felt good. Or at least better. She had no voice, and when she coughed, her head hurt, but she was ready to join the rest of the world.

Half an hour later, fresh and clean, with her long hair still damp on the ends, Christy ventured into the living room, where her mom was taking down the Christmas decorations. The tree was gone, and all the ornaments were tucked back in their boxes.

Mom looked up from where she knelt, wrapping

the figures of the nativity set in tissue and nesting them in a sturdy box. "You certainly look better."

Christy nodded.

"Still no voice?"

"It's gone," Christy whispered. "But at least it doesn't hurt to whisper like this. Would you like some help?"

"I'd love some help. Could you pull the vacuum cleaner out of the closet and try to pick up those pine needles in the corner?"

For almost an hour the two of them worked efficiently and silently. As Christy helped carry the last box out to the garage, she cleared her throat and said, "I've come up with some ideas for my wedding dress and the bridesmaids' dresses."

"I'd love to see them," Mom said. "How about if I make some soup, and you can show me what you found?"

Over chicken noodle soup, Christy showed Mom her wedding planner. "This top," she whispered in a raspy voice, "with a skirt like this. I like the wide band at the waist."

"I see," Mom said. "That would be very flattering with your small waist."

"Only I want embroidery around the bodice like this one. But with little tiny white flowers. White on white. Don't you think that would be pretty?"

"Gorgeous," Mom said. "And do you like the bodice plain like this with the ballerina-style rounded neckline and three-quarter-inch sleeves?"

Christy nodded. "I love the sleeves. Especially if they have some embroidery on them."

Her mom smiled. "I'm surprised that's what you decided on."

"Why?"

"Have you ever seen my wedding dress?"

Christy had seen pictures of her parents' wedding, but she didn't remember what her mom's wedding gown looked like. She shook her head.

"Come with me." Mom led Christy down the hallway to her bedroom, where she pulled a box from the back of the closet. It was labeled with a Wisconsin dry cleaner's advertisement.

"I remember this box," Christy said hoarsely. "I found it in your closet once when I was a little girl."

"Paula and you wanted to use it for dress-up," Mom said. "I had a fit."

"Yes, you did. I remember." Christy noticed the box had been taped shut on the right side where it had been torn. Apparently that was the side she and her childhood best friend had tried to break into.

Christy studied her mom's profile as she carefully opened the box. Christy's mom was a simple woman. Pleasantly plain in her appearance, she was shorter than Christy and rounder. Her hair had gone almost completely gray. She had never colored it. She kept it short, straight, and tucked behind her ears, which Christy thought looked better than when Mom used to wear it in what Christy called the "bubble-head hairdo" whenever they looked at old family photos.

The older Christy got, the more she admired her mom. Margaret Miller was a steady woman who always put her family first. When Christy was younger, she had longed for a peppy, outgoing mom who was more like a best friend or big sister than a mother. Her mom, however, remained the same, consistent, untrendy mom she had always been, and now Christy appreciated it. While Christy never had confided all her secrets to her mother, she had been a mom who was always available and listened with an uncritical spirit. Mom rarely offered advice. When she did, she usually had thought it through before speaking.

"Now, I want you to know," Mom began, "that this is just an idea, based on what you showed me in your pictures. I don't know if you would be interested. If you're not, please feel free to say so, because you certainly won't hurt my feelings."

Christy was beginning to feel nervous. If Mom was going to suggest Christy wear her wedding dress, Christy knew it would be a problem. Mom was shorter, for one thing. And Christy and her mom rarely shared the same taste.

"Do you see how the bodice is cut?" Mom asked, unwrapping the dress.

Christy nodded in surprise. It was the same style as the dress in the picture she had cut out. Not too scooped and slightly off the shoulders.

"These could be made into three-quarter-length sleeves," Mom said. "I know the skirt would be too short, but we could replace it with a long skirt and the wide waistband you mentioned. You could have any train length you wanted."

Christy examined the top of the dress. The scoop was just low enough to show the collarbones, and she loved the fabric. "What is this?"

"The material? I don't know. It's a blend of some sort that was very popular in my day. I don't know if my idea is any help . . ."

"May I try it on?" Christy asked.

"It will be too big on you," Mom said. "And too short."

"That's okay. I'd like to see how the top fits."

"All right."

Mom closed the bedroom door, even though they were the only ones home. Christy pulled her sweat shirt over her head and wiggled out of her jeans.

With her mom's help, Christy slid into the gown. As predicted, the dress was too big and too short, but the neckline was perfect.

"I like your idea, Mom. I would love to have your wedding gown made into my wedding gown. Are you sure you don't mind?"

Mom's face softened in a sweet smile. "Oh, Christy, I would love nothing more. Are you sure that's what you want to do?"

"Yes!" Christy pushed up the sleeves in an attempt to visualize them as three-quarter length. A cough welled up in her throat, and she turned her head and coughed for several seconds.

"It would be easy to change these into three-quarter-length sleeves," Mom said. "This will be a nice style no matter what season you finally decide on for your wedding."

Christy wondered if she should tell her mom about the potential May 22 wedding date. If she did, she would also have to explain about how she and Todd wanted the ceremony and reception in a meadow instead of a church. At this moment, she had neither the voice nor the energy to approach the complicated subject.

Fortunately, her mom went on to another topic. "I don't know if it would be hard to match the material for the skirt, but we could try. I'm sure I can buy a pattern and make the skirt. But what about the embroidered flowers? It sounded as if that was the part you liked the most about the dress you saw. I don't think I'd want to attempt embroidery. Maybe we can find someone who does that."

"I could do it," Christy said.

Mom looked surprised.

Christy cleared her throat and in a whisper said, "I never told you, but one of the things I learned in Switzerland was embroidery. I spent hours at the orphanage embroidering handkerchiefs and pillow-cases with the older girls."

"You're right, I didn't know that."

"It was a skill they could use to make salable items. Some of them were really quick and good at the details. I worked on a lot of pillowcases and a couple of tablecloths. They were finished by the girls and sold, so I didn't bring anything home that I had worked on. I think I could do it. And I think that's why the wedding gown in the magazine caught my eye. The embroidery reminded me of that year of my life."

"Let's give it a try," Mom said. "I'll take the dress apart and shorten the sleeves this weekend. You can take the bodice with you and work on the embroidery at school. If you want, we could run to the fabric store now to find a pattern and the material for the skirt. I'm sure they have a book of embroidery patterns, as well. Let me get a tape measure."

Christy stood still, with her arms outstretched. Mom measured her and estimated how much fabric they would need for the skirt.

"One thing we should both keep in mind," Mom said as she wrote down the measurements. "We should have enough time before the wedding for you to change your mind. It won't hurt my feelings if we get into this and discover it's too big of a project or if it's not turning out the way you would like."

Christy nodded. She had all kinds of optimistic thoughts about the dress turning out exactly as she wanted. Then she wondered if this was her mom's way of backing out of the project gracefully.

"Mom, if you're thinking it's too big of a challenge, we can stop. I'd hate for you to tear your wedding dress into a bunch of pieces, but then we didn't end up using it."

"We will never know unless we try," Mom said in her matter-of-fact way. "I think we can do this."

Christy gave her mom a big hug and whispered in her ear, "Thank you for sacrificing your wedding gown for me."

"It's not a sacrifice, honey. It's what I have to give. All the time you were growing up I wanted to give you so much more than we had. When Marti stepped in and treated you to so much during your teen years, I thought you would grow to resent me."

"No, Mom, not at all."

"I know my sister means well, but she called again yesterday asking if you were well enough to go up there and work on wedding plans. She reminded me that she and Bob want to pay for whatever expenses Dad and I can't cover."

Christy's heart went out to her mom, whose face had taken on a melancholy expression.

"Please don't take this to mean that your father and I don't want them to help out with the wedding. It's fine with us if she and Bob help. I know it would make them happy, and it means we can make your wedding nicer than what your father and I could afford. But I wanted to have one thing to give you that was mine."

"And you're giving me your wedding gown,"

Christy whispered warmly.

"Such as it is."

Christy smiled. "I already know that my dress will be one of my favorite parts of the wedding."

"I hope it will be." Mom's round face had a warm glow. "Actually, sweetheart, I have a feeling the favorite part of your wedding will be your honeymoon."

For the next twenty minutes, Christy and her mom sat close together on the edge of the bed. Christy was still wearing her mom's wedding dress. She sat perfectly straight, being careful not to crumple any part of it.

It struck Christy that she wasn't a little girl playing dress-up in her mommy's wedding gown, as she had once attempted to do. This was real. Not pretend. She was a woman, listening to another woman talk in hushed tones about the beauty and sanctity of giving herself to her husband on their wedding night.

Mom's choice of words was delicate. She spoke in generalities, saying she regretted that her shyness had kept her from having such an important and intimate conversation with Christy before now. Christy said she didn't know if she would have appreciated such a conversation with her mom before.

"I know that Todd and you have made wise and mature choices," Mom said. "It shows in the way you look at each other and the way you treat each other. You'll benefit from the rewards of such deep respect."

More intensely than ever Christy understood the power of virginity. Not only for Todd and her but also for their children. She realized that one day she might sit on the edge of her marriage bed with her own daughter, having this same conversation. How powerful to look her daughter in the eye, as her mother was now looking at her, and to say without a speck of regret, "Your father and I both waited for each other, and it was worth it."

With renewed determination, Christy promised herself that no matter how many months or years she and Todd had to wait until their wedding night, she would continue to save this priceless gift that could only be given once. This gift from God that would be given to only one man, a man who had saved himself for her, as well.

By the time Christy slipped out of the wedding gown and left for the fabric store with her mom, she felt as if she had met her mother for the first time. She also knew that the closeness of their newly established friendship would last for the rest of their lives.

CHRISTY AND TODD · THE COLLEGE YEARS

Christy's favorite part of her first day back on campus after Christmas vacation was having breakfast with Todd at "their" table by the window in the cafeteria. Her flu bug was gone. Her voice was back, and she had done a lot of planning over the weekend. She and Todd had talked on the phone several times after he returned from Mexico, but this was the first time they had been together in a week.

Christy had her wedding notebook with her, and the first thing she said to Todd when she sat down was, "Are you ready to get organized?"

"Organized?" Todd asked.

"For our wedding."

"Sure. I see you have a list going."

"Yes, I do." Christy turned to the first page and dived in. "We should set a time to look at rings this week. I have my wedding dress pretty well figured out, but you don't get to know anything about it or see it, so that point doesn't include you. We need to start looking at wedding invitations and to decide on the number of guests before we make a decision on the food. As soon as we have a date, we need to make airline reservations because my aunt said yesterday that some flights to Maui fill up quickly. Have you talked to the associate pastor yet about setting up our premarital counseling sessions?"

Todd leaned back and grinned broadly. "I love you."

"Don't get mushy on me." Christy pulled a pen from her backpack. "We have work to do."

Todd laughed. "Don't you think we should go to the administration office first? Then we'll know if May twenty-second is okay for us to hold the ceremony in the meadow. We can work back from there."

"Okay, but we can talk about a few things while we eat. For instance, how many attendants do you want to have? I've asked Katie to be my maid of honor, but I'm not sure who else to ask. Tracy, of course. That's assuming we get married in May. Their baby is due in July, right?"

Todd stopped eating his scrambled eggs and suspended his fork in midair. "What do you think about naming our first daughter Juliet? She could go by Julie so she wouldn't get slaughtered with Romeo jokes."

"Todd, you're getting mushy again," Christy said with half a grin. She knew Doug had discussed baby names with Todd while they were in Mexico. Todd had told her on the phone a few nights ago that Doug and he had come up with the name Daniel for the baby, if it was a boy. Christy hadn't talked to Tracy yet to find out how she felt about that name. The guys hadn't suggested a girl's name.

"I looked it up in a book Doug had," Todd continued. "Juliet means 'youthful one.' I like that. Although I've always liked Hawaiian names because of the way they sound like a little song when you say them. Maybe we could give our kids Hawaiian middle names. What do you think?"

Christy put down the pen and gave Todd a stern look. Inside, her heart was dancing. He was thinking about their children's middle names, just as she had been when she wrote him the letter last week. Maybe they weren't so opposite in their thinking after all.

With a forced expression of firm seriousness, Christy said, "Do you want to talk mushy or business? Make up your mind."

Todd laughed. "Okay, okay. Mushy later. Business now."

A grin escaped as Christy lowered her voice. "And when we do talk mushy later, you can talk as mushy as you want for as long as you want. I love it when you dream aloud."

"Dream aloud," Todd repeated. "That's what it is, isn't it? I like that, Kilikina. For so many years you and I didn't know what the future held for us so we had to keep all our dreams to ourselves. I'm glad we did that. It would have been unfair to both of us if we had started to dream aloud before we were engaged."

"I agree, Todd. You have no idea how deeply I take

dreams into my heart, and how tightly I hold on to them."

"It's the same for me," Todd said. "I would have to say that we managed to do a couple of things right. Like the piggy bank. That was a good idea."

Christy knew Todd was referring to something they had discussed months ago. Because it had been diffi-cult for them to hold back when they wanted to phys-ically express their affection for each other, they had come up with the image of each of them having a piggy bank. Whenever they wanted to give the other a kiss, they could stop and evaluate if they truly wanted to spend that kiss at that moment or to save it in the piggy bank. They knew that if they saved most of their physical expressions and spent only a tiny portion now, they both would enter their marriage wealthy in saved-up physical expressions.

"And that night after we went caroling, and you said we were at a red light—that helped me a lot," Christy said.

"It's getting more difficult, though, isn't it?" Todd asked.

Christy had a pretty good idea she knew what he was talking about, but she felt too shy to actually say it.

Todd leaned across the small corner table where they sat by the window. "It's getting more difficult, but we have to wait another 135 days."

Christy felt little bubbles of anticipation rise in her heart. "Is that how long until May twenty-second?

Only 135 more days?" She sat up straighter. "Well, then, we better get going on this list. We have a lot to do in the next 135 days."

Todd reached across the table and grasped Christy's hand before she could pick up the pen. "Come on, Kilikina, stop with the list for just a moment. Tell me, haven't you thought about it? Us becoming one? Giving ourselves to each other?"

As Christy looked into Todd's wide eyes, she was surprised she didn't feel herself blushing. This was the man she was going to marry. In 135 days, she would give herself completely to him. And they would enjoy each other for the rest of their lives. She wasn't embarrassed to think about that or to talk about it with him. It made her think of the account in Genesis that said Adam and Eve were naked and not ashamed.

Moving her chair next to Todd's, leaning close and choosing her words carefully, Christy said, "Todd, with all my heart I long to be yours. I know that I'm going to love you so completely and with so much passion that I promise you, Todd Spencer, you're going to be the happiest man who ever lived."

Todd appeared surprised and delighted with her words. Tears glistened in the corners of his eyes. He wrapped both his arms around Christy and pulled her close. Burying his face in her neck, Todd whispered into her long hair, "And I will make you the happiest woman who ever lived, my Kilikina. I promise."

As they drew apart, Christy's heart pounded so

hard it seemed to reverberate in her throat and in her ears.

"You know what? I don't think we should dream aloud about that part of our future again," Todd said in a husky voice.

Christy nodded.

"Or at least not until after we stand under our trellis in the meadow 135 days from now," Todd said firmly. He pulled back and looked at his unfinished breakfast as if he had forgotten what scrambled eggs looked like.

Christy scooted her chair back to her side of the table and took a sip of her orange juice. She doodled a flower-laced trellis at the top of the list. Their wedding arch was becoming a symbol of the passing from one stage of life into another for Todd and her.

Both of them had held on to the symbolism of a certain bridge in Hawaii that had represented life passages for them. She wondered if their wedding arch could be covered with vines and tropical flowers the way the bridge at Kipahulu had been. Todd would like that.

"Hi, kids, am I interrupting anything here?" Katie pulled up a chair to their small table. "I'll leave if you two want to be alone."

"Yeah, we want to be alone more than you can guess," Todd said. "But we'll wait 135 more days for that."

"Oh-kay." Katie glanced at Christy. "I don't think I want to know what you two were just talking about, but I have a pretty good idea."

"Have you been to our room yet?" Christy asked.

"No, I just got back on campus. I have a class in twenty minutes. I told my new boss I'd come to work early, so you probably won't see me again until after eleven tonight."

"Is today your first day at The Dove's Nest?" Todd asked.

"Yep." Katie reached for half a bagel on the corner of Todd's plate. "Are you going to eat that?"

"Help yourself. You want me to get you some eggs?" Todd offered.

Katie grinned. "Would you? You are such a sweetheart, Todd. You should have seen him in Mexico, Chris. He was Mr. Servant of All."

"Rick and you were the real heroes," Todd said, rising from his chair. "We couldn't have pulled it off if it weren't for the way you two ran the kitchen."

He walked away, and Katie turned to Christy. "What he's really saying is that it took two of us to do your job, Christy. We all missed you so much. You should have heard your honey. He talked about you constantly. All the girls in the youth group wanted to know if you were going to invite them to your wedding."

Then, glancing over her shoulder as if to make sure they were alone, Katie lowered her voice. "I have to talk to you."

Christy waited.

"Not here. Not now. Do you have any time open today before I go to work?"

"I only have two classes this morning, and I don't have to be at work in the bookstore until two."

Katie twisted her mouth in a perplexed expression. "I don't think it's going to work with my schedule. I'll just talk to you when I get back to our room tonight."

Todd returned with eggs for Katie and another bagel for himself. They chatted about how great the Mexico trip was and all the people they had met at the orphanage. Christy wished she could have gone, but she was glad for the time she had with her mom and all the planning she had done.

"I gotta fly," Katie said. "See you guys later." As she stood up, she knocked Christy's wedding notebook to the floor.

Todd and I sure didn't get very far on our to-do list.

Exactly ten hours later, Todd and Christy were seated again at their table by the window in the cafeteria. Todd was about to dig into one of his favorite handcrafted salads that resembled a green volcano with an eruption of peas flowing down the side in rivers of white ranch dressing.

"Well, I called my mom," Christy announced right after they prayed.

Todd raised an eyebrow. "What did she say?"

"She thought May twenty-second was a good choice, and she was sure Dad would agree. But when I told her we could use the meadow for the ceremony and the reception, she got real quiet."

"My dad thought it sounded great," Todd said.

"You called him already?"

Todd nodded. "I couldn't wait. I called my mom, too. I had to leave a message on her cell phone."

"Did you tell her about your graduation the end of this month? I mean, she's coming for that, too, isn't she?"

"I gave her the dates for both the graduation and the wedding. I hope it works out with her schedule."

Christy caught an edge of hurt in his words. She couldn't imagine what it must have been like for him to grow up without his mom's involvement in his life. His mother had remarried years ago and had settled with her new husband and family on the East Coast. Todd had lived with them for a short time. He rarely talked about his mother, and when he did, it was briefly and with the explanation that she had been too young when she had Todd to know how to be a mother.

"I hope she can come to both your graduation and our wedding," Christy said.

"Me too." Todd quickly moved to other topics. "What about your aunt and uncle? Did you call them?"

"No, my mom said she wanted to talk to Aunt Marti about the wedding and reception being held here. I think she felt she could commiserate with her sister since they both wanted something other than what you and I decided."

"It's our wedding," Todd said.

"I know. And I really think the meadow is the right location for us."

"It's the right location, and May twenty-second is the right date. We have a plan." Todd grinned. "So what else do you have on that check-off list of yours?"

"Would this be a good time to show you the ideas I came up with for a ring?"

"Sure."

Christy pulled the wedding planner from her backpack and turned to the pages on which she had pasted the pictures of rings and drawn a few rough sketches.

"This is the blue opal." Christy pointed to the angled, wave-like setting in the middle of a narrow gold ring.

"And it's inset, right?"

"Yes. I'd like it to be smooth with nothing raised up. On both sides, these angled insets are three tiny diamonds with three more over here." With a sense of delight she said, "See, the blue opal is like an ocean wave. The diamonds on this side are like the sand, and these are like the stars. Whenever I look at it, I'll think of how we met at the beach and how we fell in love while counting stars and walking barefoot in the sand."

Todd stared at her sketch and didn't say anything.

"What do you think?"

He looked up. "You're amazing, Kilikina. This is beautiful."

"You like it?"

"I love it. It's exactly what I would want you to

have. You've managed to fit a world of meaning into a simple band. You made it uniquely yours."

"Uniquely *ours*," Christy corrected him.

"Yes, it's uniquely ours. Should we have Mr. Frank make it for us, or do you know another jeweler you'd like to go to?"

"I think Mr. Frank would be fine. Just make sure he uses one of those deep aqua blue Australian opals with the purple and green flecks. Not the light ivory opals. I like the ones that look like the ocean."

"Got it." Todd reached for the notebook. "Mind if I take this? I can go out to Carlsbad tomorrow."

"No!" Christy grabbed the planner. "This is my brain; you can't take it from me. And you can't see the pages with my dress design on them. I'll make a copy of the ring pages and give them to you in the morning."

"Do you want to go to Carlsbad with me?" Todd asked. "You can explain your idea to Mr. Frank in person, if you want."

Christy was about to say yes because she wanted to go and she knew it would be easier for Todd if she went. But her day was already packed.

"I have to work five hours tomorrow starting at noon. I don't think I'd have time to drive to Carlsbad and be back after my eight-o'clock class. I'll write out notes for you."

"If you know what you want for your wedding band, we could have that made at the same time," Todd suggested.

"That's easy. See this picture? I cut it out of a magazine. I would like a gold band like this that's the same width as the engagement ring. What about you? What kind of wedding ring do you want?"

Todd shrugged. "I've never worn any rings. What do you think would be good?"

Christy thought a minute. She knew Todd would settle for a plain gold band and never think twice about it. But she wanted him to have something special. "How do you feel about wearing a larger version of my engagement ring?"

"Wouldn't that look kind of girly?"

"Girly?"

"Yeah, girly." Todd studied the sketches. "You know, what about having three little diamonds inset in your wedding band? Or maybe six diamonds all across the front here." He made six tiny dots with Christy's pen.

"That would be beautiful," Christy said. "But it also would be more expensive."

"That's okay."

"Would you like inset diamond chips in your band?" Christy asked.

"Nah, just a gold band would suit me."

As Christy crawled into bed that night, she thought of how easily pleased Todd was. His tastes were simple; his expectations were reasonable. He was pretty wonderful in every way. The anxiety she had experienced a few weeks ago, when she realized how poorly they communicated, seemed to be alleviated. The more time they had to sit and talk, the more helpful it was for both of them.

She glanced at the clock—11:35, and Katie wasn't back yet. Christy was more than ready to go to sleep. She had worked on embroidering her wedding gown's bodice for two hours straight before taking a shower and washing her hair. If it weren't for how eager she was to hear what Katie had to tell her, Christy would have turned out the light and crashed.

I'm sure what Katie has to tell me has something to do with Rick. Rick . . . That reminds me, Rick's letter. I never read his letter.

Climbing out of bed, Christy pulled her suitcase from the back of her closet and ran her hand through the inside pockets. She found the crumpled envelope. Instead of returning to her warm bed, she coaxed herself over to the surfboard sofa and attempted to make friends with the beast by sitting down and leaning against the cold backrest. She tucked her feet underneath her and tried to get comfortable.

Opening the envelope, Christy pulled out two folded pieces of stationery. A hundred-dollar bill floated to her lap. Her surprised eyes quickly scanned the handwritten letter.

Dear Christy,

I hope I can hand this to you in person one day because that way I'll be able to see your eyes, and I'll know if you really have forgiven me for taking your gold bracelet. I think I already know that you've forgiven me, but it will help if I see it in your eyes.

The enclosed money is to reimburse you for what you had to pay to redeem your bracelet from the jewelers. If it's more than you had to pay, then use it for something else. Just promise me that you'll accept it as restitution for my foolish actions.

As you probably know by now, God has gotten ahold of my life. I still can't believe He didn't give up on me long ago. He patiently brought me back to himself, and I'm a different person. It's all God's doing, not mine.

What you don't know is that you were there on a significant day in my life. I didn't know it at the time, but God used an object lesson to get my attention years later. I'm referring to the first Sunday you visited our church and sat with me in class. Do you remember how the teacher had Katie stand on a chair and how he dubbed me "Peter Pagan"? "Katie Christian" tried to pull me up to her with no success. Then, with one little tug, I pulled her down to my level.

Well, I never forgot that. I realized that I had gone through my life pulling others down. When I finally hit the bottom, I kept remembering how vulnerable Katie was when I pulled her off that chair. I realized I didn't have the kind of trusting relationship she had expressed with anyone. I knew I wanted to have that kind of trust in the Lord. I had sort of made a business deal with Him. You know, I told Him I'd follow the rules if He would keep me out of hell. But it doesn't work that way. I found out He wanted all of me. He wanted me to open my heart and to receive Him fully. And once I repented, that's what happened.

So please accept this restitution and know that I'm sorry for the way I treated you.

Your brother in Christ,
Rick Doyle

Before Christy had a chance to respond to the letter, the door opened, and Katie entered holding a bright bouquet of mixed flowers. Her face glowed.

"Well," Christy said, "must have been a good first day at your job."

"My boss gave these to me."

"Nice welcome present."

"Rick doesn't give flowers to every new employee." Katie was still standing by the closed door, as if she were caught in a dream and unable to move forward.

"No, I wouldn't imagine he does."

"I don't know what to do with them."

"They probably would like some water," Christy suggested.

Katie swallowed and gave Christy a shy smile.

"What?" Christy asked.

Katie drew the bouquet to her blushing face and sniffed its fragrance. With a twinkle in her shimmering green eyes, she said in a very small voice, "I really like him. I mean, really, really."

Christy said, "Oh? Really?"

"Yes, really."

"Christy, I never expected this." Katie sat down on the surfing sofa and held the flowers in her lap. "It's only been a few weeks, but did you know that we've seen each other every day since you and Todd got engaged? Rick and I talk about everything. We had a great time together in Mexico, and Christmas was wonderful with his family. His mom loves me. His dad told me on New Year's Eve I was a gift from God to their son." Tears rolled down Katie's cheeks.

Christy was waiting for the bad news. "So, what was it you wanted to talk to me about this morning? In the cafeteria you said—"

"What's that?" Katie looked at Rick's letter that Christy had left on the sofa.

"The letter Rick gave me. Go ahead, read it."

Katie scanned the letter. She looked up at Christy with searching eyes. "What is God doing?"

Christy smiled. "My best friend, Katie, would call this a huge God-thing."

"This is beyond huge. It's mind-bending. And God is doing it, not me. I don't want to run ahead, or get freaked and pull back. I just want to take each step as it comes and to be right in line with what God has for me. For us. I want God to fulfill His purpose for me."

Christy tried not to let out a cheer for her impulsive friend, who was showing more caution and wise thinking than Christy had ever seen in her. Instead, Christy just nodded support and understanding.

"Yesterday Rick said that having me in his life has been like the song Doug was working on. Rick said that when the Lord brought us together, his life filled with joy and laughter. The flowers are a thank-you to me for being me. But I got nervous and thought maybe he was trying to tell me that our relationship was about to go to the next level, you know?"

"So what did you tell him?"

"I opened my mouth like only I can, and I told him exactly what I was thinking."

Christy knew that Katie could be pretty brutal when she decided to be honest. Wincing slightly, she waited to hear Katie's report.

"I told Rick I trusted him with our friendship. I told him I didn't want either of us to make judgments based on the past. I forgave him when his letter came, and I truly know that I did. I don't harbor anything against him in my heart. But I told him I'm not inter-ested in a speedy relationship."

Katie looked at Christy with self-doubt all over her face. "Then I said, 'If there's anything lasting that's going to grow out of our friendship, then it will be here five months from now or a year from now or ten years from now.' "

Christy's eyes grew wide. "How did he react to that?"

"He said he felt the same way. He said he was interested in a friendship that would last forever, no matter what. He had no expectations of me and wasn't in a hurry to make any predictions about what God was doing in our lives."

"That's wonderful."

"I know. So tell me I said the right thing."

Christy sat next to Katie, putting her arm around Katie's shoulders. "Of course you did the right thing. You're an amazing, strong, incredible woman, and you handled what could have been an awkward situation with honesty and integrity."

Katie smiled slowly, followed by a rhythmic nodding of her head. "Yeah, I did, didn't I? For once in my life I did the right thing."

"You do a lot of things right."

"Not when it comes to guys. You know my long list of failures in that arena better than anyone. And if by any remote chance this guy is the one I'm going to end up spending the rest of my life with, I want to make sure I don't go crazy and make all my decisions on impulse. I don't want to run ahead of God."

Christy gave Katie a glowing smile. "You are absolutely amazing."

"Amazing nothing! I'm exhausted! Do you know

how much emotional energy I've spent in the last twenty-four hours processing my feelings, starting a new job working for him, and trying to figure out how I was going to tell you all this?"

"I hope you expected me to be supportive."

"I didn't know what you would think."

"I think God is doing His God-thing. Katie, you deserve the best, and I only want God's best for you. For both of you. That's all I've ever wanted."

"I know," Katie said quietly. She sat next to Christy and let out a deep sigh. "Chris, I have to tell you something. I know I should have told you a long time ago, but things changed in both of our lives, and I decided to let it go. However, in light of what's been happening with Rick during these past few weeks, I think I better tell you."

Christy couldn't imagine any secret Katie could have kept from her, let alone a secret she had kept for a number of years.

"Do you remember the night we went to the sleepover at Janelle's when we were sophomores?"

"Yes, of course."

"Do you remember how we all went out that night and T.P.'d Rick's house? You didn't run fast enough, and we took off in the motor home. You were left hiding in the bushes."

"Katie, of course I remember all this. Rick's dad sent him outside to clean up the toilet paper. I jumped out of the bushes, and Rick chased me down the street."

"Right. And that's when Rick became obsessed with you."

"I wouldn't say he was obsessed with me."

"Well, that's how I saw it," Katie said. "Now, this is the part that's hard for me to tell you. I thought then that if I became your friend, I could get closer to Rick, and that's pretty much what I did."

Christy let Katie's words sink in.

"I used you, Christy. I've wanted to apologize to you for years, but it got kind of complicated."

"That's okay. I never felt as if you used me."

"That's because you welcomed me into your life. I had never had a best friend before, and I ended up wanting to be your friend more than I wanted Rick to notice me. So I told myself I didn't care about Rick. The truth is," Katie said slowly, "I was being eaten alive with jealousy."

"You never showed it."

"Oh yes I did. You're being gracious, Christy. I struggled all the time, and you know it. When you dumped Rick, half of me cheered that you took a stand and let him know what a jerk he had been to you. The other half of me hoped I might finally have a chance to get him to notice me. How sick is that?"

"I don't think it's sick, Katie. I think it's honest. It's complicated, like you said. Everything was a lot more confusing in high school."

"I wish I had talked to you about all of this back then. There never seemed to be a good time. I almost said something during the spring of our junior year, when we went to visit the guys at their apartment in San Diego."

Katie paused and then leaned forward before continuing her confession. "Actually, I should go back to January of that year, when we went to the Rose Parade. Rick kissed me at midnight—you know that. It was a spontaneous Happy New Year's kiss. A big nothing for him. But it was my first kiss, and it was with Rick, and it was huge for me."

Christy hung her head. "And I gave you a hard time about it."

"Hey, this is my confession, not yours. Your heart was in the right place. You didn't want me to get hurt. But I did get hurt. And then when we stayed at Stephanie's next to the guys' apartment in San Diego, Rick walked me to the door late that night. He kissed me, and I kissed him back. I never told you."

"I knew," Christy said softly.

Katie turned with a surprised look on her face. "You knew? Why didn't you say anything?"

"It was awkward, like you said."

"Yes, it was. I gave Rick plenty of opportunities the next day at the zoo to make good on his kiss and to express interest in me. But he was a blob."

"That was pretty awful," Christy agreed.

"Do you remember what you said to me in front of the koala bears at the zoo?"

"In front of the koala bears? No, I have absolutely no idea what I said to you in front of the koala bears."

"You made me promise you something. You said,

'Promise me you won't let Rick use you.' "

"I don't remember that."

"Well, I do, because your advice cut me in half. I knew that's what I had done with you in the beginning. I had used you to get to Rick. I confessed it to God right then and got my heart right with Him, but I was too chicken to confess everything to you and ask you to forgive me. But I want to ask your forgiveness now, Chris. I'm so sorry."

"Katie, I forgive you. Please don't worry about that. It was complicated, like you said. I never held any of this against you."

"I know you didn't. But I still had to get it off my chest. You have this way about you, Christy. You open your heart, and you make people feel as if they can mosey on in, take off their shoes, and stay awhile. That's what I did back in high school and, well, here we are. Still friends."

"Best of friends," Christy echoed.

"I guess a couple of peculiar treasures like us don't come along every day, do they?"

"Definitely not." Christy paused before adding, "And a God-lover like Rick Doyle doesn't come along every day, either."

Katie stared at her hands.

"Let me pray for you. For us." Christy placed a comforting hand on Katie's shoulder and thanked God for what He had done in their lives in the past and for what He was doing now and would do in the future.

She prayed for wisdom for Katie and Rick and for direction for Todd and her.

Katie prayed, as well. They hugged and both cried a little. Then Katie went to the laundry room, where she found a plastic pitcher and filled it with water for her flowers. It was almost two in the morning when Christy finally coaxed Katie to turn out the light.

In the dark stillness of their room, Katie said, "I didn't tell you one other thing."

Christy was almost asleep and didn't think she could handle any more surprise announcements or confessions.

"We haven't kissed yet," Katie said simply.

Christy opened her eyes and stared across the dark room at Katie's bed. All she saw was the silhouette of Naranja's top curve.

"Rick told me he made a promise to God that he would clean up his act in that area. He wanted me to know, as our relationship progressed, that he would be taking it really slow in physical expression. I think that's a good choice. For him. For us. It takes a lot of the pressure off, you know? Well, I just thought I'd tell you. Good night."

"Good night." Christy rolled over on her side. Now she was wide awake with not-so-pleasant memories of when she had dated Rick, before his act was cleaned up. Christy was fifteen. She was trusting and inexperienced. Rick was direct and expressive. She knew that the handful of kisses Rick had stolen had been part of what she forgave him for a long time ago. As the unsettled feelings now tried to come back and torment her, she reminded herself that it was in the past. It was forgiven. Forgotten. Erased from God's book. Buried in the deepest sea.

A saying came to mind. *"When the enemy comes knocking on a door you closed long ago, you just call out, 'Jesus, it's for you!' "*

Christy smiled. She pulled up the covers to her chin and let Jesus answer the door while she floated off to dreamland.

Three weeks later the saying came to her again. This time Todd heard the enemy knocking on a door he thought he had closed long ago.

It was the evening of Todd's graduation. Christy's parents, her brother, her aunt and uncle, and Todd's dad all had come to cheer for him when he received his diploma. Christy took a roll of film of Todd in his cap and gown and handed her camera to David to take several shots of Christy and Todd together. Katie, Rick, Sierra, and a bunch of other friends came from school. Christy made sure they all posed in a group picture with her favorite graduate.

Afterward, a group of eleven family and friends went to a steak house in town. Todd's dad treated them to a fabulous dinner in a private room. The day had been filled with cheers, laughter, and applause. Christy thought it couldn't have gone better.

Yet, as Todd drove Christy back to the dorm, she could tell he was upset or sad about something by the way his shoulders slumped. Christy reached over and gave his arm three squeezes. A slow grin of appreciation came to his face. He glanced over at Christy.

"You know," he said, turning his attention back to the road, "I thought she couldn't hurt me anymore. I thought I was over it. But when my mom called yesterday and said she wasn't coming, I found myself remembering every important event in my life she's missed. She was really never there for me. Ever."

Christy felt her heart go out to him.

"Except when I was born, of course." He lightened his tone, as if trying to make a joke. "I guess that one was mandatory."

During the past month, ever since Christy had tried on her mom's wedding dress, she and her mom had become closer than ever. They spoke on the phone almost every day and were working closely together on all the wedding details. She couldn't imagine what it would be like to have a mother who would call at the last minute to say she found it "inconvenient" to come to Christy's college graduation.

"I was thinking about that quote you told me a few weeks ago about asking the Lord to answer the door when the enemy comes knocking," Todd said. "I guess that's what I need to do in this situation. It's a door of hurt and disappointment that I shut long ago when I forgave her. It's not a door I should open again."

"It might be," Christy said cautiously.

"What do you mean?"

"You know how last week in our premarital counseling session Pastor Ross said we should feel free to discuss with him any areas of our lives that we think might be a challenge after we're married? Well, I think this might be a challenge for you, for us, for the rest of our lives. It might help to talk openly to someone about it."

"Maybe," Todd said.

"Do you think your mom will come to our wedding?"

"I don't know. In a way, I don't know if I want her there. I know this is going to sound crazy, but I'd almost rather have Bob and Marti sit in the front row where my parents normally would sit."

"I'm sure they would be honored if you asked them. I know they both feel like you're a son to them. But what about your dad?"

"I asked him to be my best man."

"You did?" It was the first Christy had heard of it. She had listed Doug as Todd's best man in the wedding planner, but then she didn't remember Todd and her ever talking specifics. She had just assumed.

"Is that allowed in the world of wedding etiquette? Can you have your dad stand up as your best man?" Todd pulled into the parking lot behind Christy's dorm and parked the Volvo.

"I don't know. We keep saying it's our wedding, so I guess we can do whatever we want."

"My dad always has been there for me. He's the first person I thought of. I want him to stand beside me."

"Okay," Christy said. "I think that's great." Her mind was busy rearranging details that had been penciled in her notebook. "You and I should set aside some time this week to work on our plans. My aunt gave me some wedding invitation samples today."

"I saw her hand them to you. Do you like any of them?"

"Not really. I'd prefer it if you and I could go to a stationery store and look at more samples together. We have to decide on the wording, and Marti said that she arranged for an artist friend of hers to address the invitations in calligraphy, but she needs six weeks to do them. The invitations need to be sent out six weeks to a month before the wedding. If it takes a month to print them, we're almost out of time already."

"You're starting to sound panicked," Todd said. "There's no need to panic. We can go sometime this week, just not on Monday. That's when I start my new job."

"What new job?"

"Painting houses."

Christy didn't try to hide the shocked expression on her face this time. "What job painting houses?"

"I didn't tell you?"

"No."

"A guy at church asked if I wanted a part-time job helping him paint houses since the position at church is only part time until June. I told him I could start as soon as I graduated. It's only thirty hours a week."

"Todd, that's a lot."

"The money is good. We need it, Christy. I can work flexible hours around my schedule at church. It won't interfere with our counseling sessions on Tuesdays, and I have weekends off. Are you sure I didn't tell you about this?"

"I think I would remember." Christy adjusted her position in the passenger's seat. "This is exactly the kind of thing I was talking about last week at counseling when Ross asked if I felt any areas needed to be addressed right away. You don't tell me things, Todd."

"I thought I told you about this job."

"I don't remember ever hearing about it until this minute." Her voice was elevating. "And this is the first time you said anything about your dad being your best man."

"I didn't think it would be a problem," Todd said. "We have plenty of time before the wedding to do all this planning."

"Not if you're going to be working sixty hours a week!"

"It's not sixty hours. It's thirty for the painting job and twenty at church."

"Todd, you work more than twenty hours a week at church. You're there for meetings and on call whenever one of the teens or a parent wants to talk to you about something. Like last week when you never showed up for dinner because you took some of the guys skateboarding and ended up talking to one of them until eleven o'clock."

"That's how youth ministry goes sometimes. He had a lot of questions about God."

"I know." Christy tried to pull herself down a notch

and be more understanding. "And that's what you're good at. I just want to make sure I'm still on your list of priorities once you start working a second job."

"You're at the very top," Todd said.

"Then you give me a time when we can look at invitations this week."

Todd seemed to be flipping through an invisible calendar in his mind. "What about next Saturday. I could meet you after the men's prayer breakfast at church."

"Next Saturday is the soonest you could go with me?"

"You could go by yourself or with Katie or somebody and find what you like and then show it to me. I don't have a strong preference on the invitations."

Christy felt herself about to boil over. Usually she swallowed her frustration and went along with whatever Todd suggested. Not this time. If she was going to learn to communicate with her future husband, it would be now or never.

"No, Todd!" she spouted. "I don't want to go shopping with Katie or my mom or anyone else. This is *our* wedding, and you need to participate in the planning. It makes me so mad when you sit back and expect me to do everything!"

"Okay, okay!" Todd held up a hand, as if to hold back the force of her words. "When do you want to go shopping for invitations?"

"I don't know," Christy said sullenly. She didn't like the way she felt right now. "Saturday, I guess, if that's the soonest you're available."

"Okay," Todd said. "Saturday. Around eleven. Is that okay with you?"

"Fine."

"Okay."

"Okay." Christy drew in a deep breath and tried not to burst into tears.

Am I going to have to wrestle you to the ground on everything that's important to me for the rest of our lives, Todd? We have to communicate better. I'm still mad; you're mad. When do things get better for us instead of worse?

CHRISTY AND TODD · THE COLLEGE YEARS

The first week of February turned out to be one of the worst weeks of Christy's life but, strangely, one of the best weeks, too.

11 On Monday she started classes for her last semester, only to find that one of the classes she needed to graduate had been cancelled. To take the class at the only other offered time meant re-adjusting her work schedule at the campus bookstore. She was cut back from twelve hours a week to eight, which meant less money.

On Tuesday, Todd didn't show up for their second premarital counseling session at church. He left a message with Pastor Ross saying he couldn't break away from his painting job and to please tell Christy he was sorry, but he would be there for sure next Tuesday.

Christy was stuck at church because she had gotten a ride there with Katie and then expected Todd to take her back to school. She decided against staying with Pastor Ross and discussing anything because she was so mad at Todd, she was certain she would later regret anything she said in the counseling session. She hadn't figured out how to express her feelings without exploding in a burst of pent-up fury.

Being too upset and too proud to ask for a ride back to campus, Christy decided to walk the five miles. She had walked everywhere during her year at school in Switzerland and felt certain the trek would help her to release her anger. All it gave her were blisters and more anger toward Todd for putting his job above her.

She rehearsed all kinds of conversations she planned to have with Todd once he showed his face. None of them were pretty.

To make matters worse, Todd didn't call her Tuesday night. Since he had moved in with Rick the day before he graduated, each time Christy called, she got Rick's voice mail. Finally she gave up and went to bed early. Katie was at work, and Christy was too upset to do homework or to embroider her wedding dress bodice.

Wednesday morning the phone rang at 6:30. Christy was certain Todd was calling with an apology. But it was her mom, and her voice was low.

"Grandpa passed away last night," she said. "He had been complaining of stomach pains, and Grandma took him to the hospital yesterday afternoon. He died while they were doing exploratory surgery."

Christy already felt drained. This news sent her into a flood of tears. She loved her grandparents and suddenly regretted that she hadn't seen them since their fiftieth wedding anniversary back in Wisconsin the summer after she graduated from high school.

Marti called an hour later and said she had plane tickets reserved for Todd and Christy to attend the funeral on Saturday.

Friday night Todd and Christy took a red-eye flight with her parents, her brother, and Bob and Marti. They landed at O'Hare airport in Chicago at five o'clock in the morning. Their connecting flight to Madison left at six. After renting a van, they drove through a light snowstorm for three hours, arriving in Christy's hometown of Brightwater, Wisconsin, only a half hour before the funeral.

Christy and Todd hadn't talked about their unresolved tension. She was still upset with him, but those feelings had been set aside to deal with the grief of her grandfather's death.

Todd was the perfect gentleman as he met Christy's relatives for the first time. She knew her grandma was taken with him, even in the midst of her grief and shock.

Marti was on a mission to stay in Wisconsin until she had grilled every doctor and hospital staff member involved in caring for her father. She was certain his death was unnecessary and the result of human error. Instead of grieving her father's death, the way Christy's mom was, Marti was fighting for justice.

"It won't bring Grandpa back," David said as they stood around in the living room at Grandma's house after the funeral.

Everyone stared at him. David wasn't the sort to

speak up in a group about anything.

"It will make things right," Marti declared. "And that's important in this world."

"But Grandpa isn't in this world anymore. He's in heaven," David said. "You'll see him again if you give your life to the Lord like I did."

Christy stared at her little brother. He sounded just like Todd. She could tell David's evaluation of the situation was the last thing Marti wanted to hear. She made a swift exit. Christy wasn't surprised to see Todd follow Marti. While Todd talked to Marti, Christy prepared to leave.

The rest of her family planned to stay in Brightwater until Monday, but Christy and Todd had a flight back that night so Todd could be at church in the morning. The snow had stopped, and Christy's grandma said she was certain the main roads would be plowed so they should make it to the airport just fine.

With their brief visit almost over, Christy wanted to have a special moment with her grandma. She drew her grandmother into the hallway, took her hands, and spoke condolences softly, telling her grandma how much she loved her.

"Thank you, precious. And thank you for coming all this way."

"I wish we could stay longer."

"No," Grandma said. "There will be so much commotion here for the next few days. Todd and you will have to come another time to see me when you can stay for a nice little visit. I would like that."

"You will come to our wedding in May, won't you?"

"I wouldn't miss it for anything. You have a real gem there, Christina. I'm happy for you both."

"Thank you, Grandma." Christy gave her grandmother's cool hands a squeeze. "Do you have any advice for me? For us?"

Christy was remembering her grandparents' fiftieth wedding anniversary party when she had asked them how they had met and how they had known they were right for each other. Her grandfather had offered some advice about making sure they came from the same background. Grandma, however, had told Christy to wait until things were difficult and then to ask herself if she still wanted to spend the rest of her life with this person.

That thought had come back to Christy several times during the past week while she was mad at Todd. She knew she still wanted to spend the rest of her years with him. She just wanted to get along better with Todd.

"It goes very fast." A tear glistened in Grandma's eye before finding its way down her wrinkled cheek. "It's over so soon. Keep short lists, honey. Learn to forgive quickly and go on because one day you'll wake up and find that somehow you got old when you weren't looking. Your lists won't matter at all then."

Christy wrapped her arms around her sweet grandmother and held her close in a warm hug. She could feel her grandma shaking as she sobbed quietly into Christy's shoulder. Tears flooded Christy's eyes.

She blinked them away and noticed a photograph only a few inches away from her. The hallway in which they stood was one long family photo gallery. The photo in front of Christy was a picture of her parents' wedding. Her mom was wearing the dress that now had been dissected to create Christy's wedding dress. Her parents looked so young. Mom had rich brown hair that fell gracefully onto her shoulders, and Dad stood tall, strong, and straight. Beside her parents stood Christy's grandmother and grandfather, dressed in their finest and smiling wildly.

For the first time, it really struck her that her grandfather was gone. She drew her grandmother closer and cried her eyes out.

Several hours later, when Christy and Todd were in their seats and the airplane was taking off, Todd took Christy's hand in his. He drew it to his lips and tenderly kissed the back of her hand again and again. She leaned her head against his shoulder and cried some more.

For the first half of the flight, they didn't speak. Todd had lifted the armrest between them, and they sat as close as they could, with her head on his shoulder and his head resting on hers. She stopped counting the number of times he pressed his lips to her hair, showering her with tiny kisses like snowflakes that melted as soon as they touched her.

Christy studied Todd's hands. The wounds from his horrible car accident had healed, but the scars remained. For the rest of his life, Todd would bear the marks of the places where the shattered glass had pierced his skin. Christy traced the scars with her fingers, as if her homework assignment were to memorize each wound.

When they finally spoke to each other, Todd's deep voice rumbled through her ear all the way to her heart. "I'm sorry," he whispered.

Christy pulled up her head so she could face him. They were only inches apart as she whispered, "We're going to get old, Todd. We're going to get old together. Lord willing, we'll have fifty years or more like my grandparents did. When it comes to things that upset me, I promise to keep a short list. I'm determined to learn how to communicate with you in a way that allows me to express my opinion, but kindly. Love is patient and kind, right? I'm also determined to learn how to forgive you quickly. I don't ever want to hold as much against you as I have this week."

Todd stroked her cheek. A funny little expression played across his eyes.

"What were you just thinking?" Christy asked.

Todd looked into her eyes. "I said I was sorry because I was thinking about your grandfather. I didn't realize you had been mad at me all week."

Christy paused before answering. This was a good time for her to practice speaking the truth in love. "I was mad that you missed our counseling session. I'm not mad anymore."

"What about the invitations?" Todd asked.

"What about them?"

"We missed our appointment to look at invitations this morning," Todd said.

"We can look next week. Or I can look and tell you what I've found. Or you can look and tell me what you found. I have to learn to be more flexible."

"And I have to learn to be more dependable."

"Okay," Christy said with a tender smile.

"Okay." Todd returned the smile. His lips traveled the tiny distance that separated them, and he met her mouth with a warm kiss.

"Excuse me," the flight attendant said, leaning toward them. "Did you want chicken or lasagna?"

Christy straightened herself and made a quick decision. "Chicken."

"I'll have the same," Todd echoed.

As they ate, they discussed their busy schedules and how they could find more time to be together. This semester was the fullest for Christy, and as she had predicted, Todd often worked more than fifty hours a week. They talked about what could be adjusted in both their schedules and ended up coming to the same conclusion. Every Saturday would be theirs. Their weekly schedules left them little time to see each other, so every Saturday between then and Saturday, May 22, would be set aside for them to do whatever they wanted or needed to do together.

"Do you realize," Todd said, "that's only thirteen Saturdays? Or is it fourteen?" He moved his fingers as he recounted.

"It's not a lot, no matter how many it is," Christy

said. "Whatever I can do without you, I'll try to do. I'll make certain I tell you all the details, though."

"Are you sure that will be all right? Because I can try to adjust things if you want me to go along shopping or something."

"No, it doesn't bother me now that I have a more realistic view. I was being sentimental, thinking we should do everything together and trying to make a memory out of every wedding detail. I've watched too many movies. This is reality. You're working fifty hours a week so we'll have enough money to eat after we're married; I'm finishing my toughest semester so far and working part time. We have to make adjustments."

"Your mom and your aunt are dying to be involved and do more of the planning. Can you delegate some things to them?"

Christy handed her finished meal tray to the flight attendant and closed her tray table. Todd did the same.

"You're right," Christy said. "I'll go down the list and delegate like crazy as soon as they get back from Wisconsin."

"Good. Do we have plans already for what we're going to work on next Saturday?"

Christy wasn't sure how to answer that. It was the weekend before Todd's birthday, and she had been thinking about a party for him. Nothing had been arranged yet, but she wanted to have a big surprise party.

"I'm not sure yet," she answered.

"I thought maybe you and I could go to the beach for the day. We could cook breakfast on the beach, and

I could try out the surfboard my dad gave me for Christmas."

"It's February," Christy said. "Won't it be cold?"

"Yes."

She knew that was a poor excuse if she was trying to dissuade him. He hadn't been surfing for months, and she realized he was eager to get back in the water. They had cooked their breakfast on the beach in cold weather more than once. Christy decided to come right out with it.

"It's right before your birthday, and I—"

"I know. That's why I want to go. Just you and me. Breakfast on the beach. What do you say, Kilikina? That's all I want for my birthday."

Christy decided not to mention the plans she had been formulating for his surprise party. Todd's idea of a memorable party obviously was a private affair.

"Sounds perfect," Christy said. "I'll organize the food."

"That's what I was counting on." Todd reached for her hand, stroking her Forever ID bracelet with his thumb.

They were quiet a minute while Christy readjusted details in her mind. It could work. She could stay at her aunt and uncle's, and she and Todd could have an early breakfast. That would leave them the entire afternoon to look at wedding cakes and invitations and—

"Kilikina," Todd murmured, breaking into her planning. He drew her hand to his lips and kissed her ring finger. "I just decided something."

"What?"

Todd adjusted his position and reached into the back pocket of his jeans. He pulled out a wadded-up tissue and held it in his hand.

"I was going to do this on the way home from my graduation dinner, but neither of us was in a very good mood that night. Then I thought I'd take you to a fancy restaurant this weekend, but here we are on an airplane eating chicken. If I were a patient man, I'd wait till next Saturday on the beach or come up with a special plan for Valentine's Day. But I've waited too long, and I'm too eager for you to have this."

Todd unfolded the wad of tissue, and there, in the crumpled nest in his hand, sat Christy's engagement ring.

"Marry me, Kilikina." Todd slipped the ring on Christy's finger. "Marry me and grow old with me."

At that moment, flying thirty thousand feet somewhere over Colorado, Christy knew more deeply and more profoundly than ever that she always would be in love with Todd Spencer. The intensity of her love for him at that second made it seem as if she hadn't even begun to love him until now.

"Yes," she whispered. "I will marry you."

They kissed a long, slow, promise-sealing kiss.

Christy glanced at her hand on which she now wore a glorious, one-of-a-kind engagement ring. "It's beautiful."

"Yeah, I was real happy with how it turned out. It fits you perfectly."

"Yes, it does. In every way."

Even though they had been engaged before this moment, and even though Christy never had thought she needed a ring to prove she was promised to Todd, the ring seemed to change everything for her. It reminded her that one day very soon she and Todd would become man and wife. It also was evidence to everyone who noticed it that she was taken. She was going to be given in marriage very soon. She was loved and desired and waiting for her wedding day.

Christy jotted all those thoughts in her diary on Thursday night of that week. Katie still wasn't back from work, which was typical. Things still were moving along at a steady pace with Rick and Katie, and she seemed happier than ever.

With Katie gone so often and Todd not around on campus for Christy to meet in the cafeteria for meals, she found herself spending a lot of quiet time in her dorm room doing homework, working on her embroidery, and thinking.

At ten o'clock that night, Christy put away her embroidery and crawled into bed, full of thoughts. She pulled out her diary to record what Todd had said to the group of teenagers he had taught Sunday morning. He had told them about giving Christy her ring on the plane the night before and how her face had lit up.

> *Then Todd made the most incredible analogy between us being engaged and the way God views us. In the Bible God describes the church as the Bride of Christ. Todd said the Holy Spirit is like the engagement ring that God gives us as evi-*

dence of His promise that He will always love us and one day will come and take us to be His bride to live with Him forever.

It was amazing the way the students responded. Todd said that weddings on earth are a reflection of the great wedding feast of the Lamb that will happen when the Lord comes to take His bride, the Church, to be with Him.

I realized more deeply what a mystery that is. I felt so different and so much more in love with Todd after he placed the ring on my finger. I find myself growing more deeply in love with Christ as I see these parallels acted out in my life. Christ wants me and is waiting for me one day to be with Him forever. Until that day, His Holy Spirit in my life is evidence to others that I am promised to Him and I am waiting for Him.

That verse in Ephesians 4:30 makes more sense to me than it ever did before. "Do not grieve the Holy Spirit of God, with whom you were sealed for the day of redemption." Todd told the class it would be like my covering my ring finger with duct tape because I didn't want anyone to know I was engaged. He said that as my fiancé, it would break his heart if I did that. Yet we do the same thing when we don't let the Holy Spirit work in our lives.

Todd's charge to the class was to boldly let the whole world know that we're spoken for, that we belong to Christ. Then he said, "But if you're really in love with the Bridegroom, people will know instantly when they look at your face. Just look at Christy."

The whole group turned to stare at me, but I didn't care. My face and my heart were so brightly lit on fire with my love for God and Todd that I didn't feel at all embarrassed. I felt as if I were floating on clouds.

Christy stopped writing for a moment and

thought about how clouds figured into the future of all Christians everywhere.

That's what's going to happen when Christ comes for His bride, isn't it? He's going to meet us in the clouds.

Her thoughts reminded her of a certain magnificent early morning, when she and Todd had met in the chapel and had walked in the meadow. She had felt as if the clouds had come to earth that morning.

Reaching for her Bible, Christy looked up all the references to clouds she could find. She remembered 1 Thessalonians 4:17 was the one about being caught up in the clouds and meeting the Lord in the air. A lump grew in her throat as she read the last part of the verse and underlined it. "And so we will be with the Lord forever."

Christy grabbed her diary and wrote,

> *Todd was right about what he said to the teens. My brother was right about what he said to Aunt Marti after the funeral. My grandma was right, too. What we're doing here isn't about this life only. The real us, our souls, will last forever. God wants us to say yes to His Son so we can be with Him forever. It's the ultimate "I do." The eternal "I promise."*

Overwhelmed by the intense insights, Christy put away her diary and turned out the light. Then quietly, she turned her face into her pillow and cried. Part of her tears were a good-bye and I'll-see-you-in-heaven to her grandfather; part were for her joyous love for Todd; part were for the mystery of

God's loving her and wanting her to be with Him forever. The final batch of tears was for her aunt, who still hadn't said yes to Christ. Christy knew that according to God's Word, Aunt Marti wouldn't be with Him forever unless she surrendered her heart to Him.

The door opened, and Katie slipped in, humming. "You awake?" she whispered.

"Hmm," Christy responded. She didn't want Katie to turn on the overhead light and keep Christy up talking all night. Yet, if Katie had any big announcements to make, Christy didn't want to miss them.

"I'm leaving early in the morning for the Natural Food Fest in San Diego. Rick is picking me up at six. I just wanted you to know."

"Mmm-hmm," Christy answered.

"Are you okay?"

"Mmm-hmm."

"Good. Everything is going great with Rick. I'll see you sometime tomorrow night."

"Mmm-hmm."

Christy fell asleep to the happy sound of Katie humming her way into her pajamas.

The calendar that hung on Christy's wall in her dorm room stared back innocently at her as she tried to find some white space to write down her scheduled trip to the dentist. She had made the appointment at work that afternoon without the benefit of consulting her crowded calendar.

"March twelve," she muttered to herself. "How did it get to be March twelve already? If I go to the dentist at four o'clock next Tuesday, that means I'll be late for our counseling appointment at church."

Christy chewed on the end of her pen and tried to decide if she should ask Todd for the car that day or for him to take off from work to drive her to the dentist. They could reschedule their counseling appointment for a little later.

Christy was trying hard to remain flexible. It was getting more and more difficult to coordinate schedules, what with Todd working so much. The past few weeks had flown by. The only fun time the two of

them had managed to fit in was their Saturday breakfast on the beach. The morning had turned out to be
clear, crisp, and sunny, and they had enjoyed every
minute of it. Christy had bought fifteen small gifts that
she had wrapped for Todd. He opened the first one at
seven o'clock while the bacon was sizzling over the
dancing fire. It was wax for his surfboard.

From then on, every hour on the hour, she gave
Todd another little present until nine o'clock that
night. The last gift was a picture of the two of them
that Tracy had taken years ago on the beach. They were
sitting with the rest of the gang, and the late-after-
noon sun shone on their faces just right. Tracy had
captured them on film at the very second Todd and
Christy were exchanging glances. Their expressions
were lit up with the glimmer of wonder and joy at the
birth of first love.

Christy didn't remember the picture being taken,
but the morning they had eaten omelets at Doug and
Tracy's, Tracy had pulled it out of a photo album and
given it to Christy.

She loved the picture and had made a special mat
for it by gluing on dried, browned carnation petals ex-
tracted from the first bouquet Todd had given her. The
flowers had been stored for more than five years in an
old Folgers coffee can and smelled a little funny. In her
nicest printing, Christy had written at the bottom of
the mat, *I hold you in my heart. Forever, Your Kilikina.*

Todd got choked up when he opened his final gift
and stared at the picture. "We were so young." Then he

held Christy close and told her this was the best birthday he had ever had.

The warm memories of that special day had been
Christy's only company in the midst of her overly full
schedule. The only good thing was that the time was
going by quickly.

Every free moment Christy had, she spent working
on embroidering her wedding gown. She nearly was
finished with the string of tiny white forget-me-nots
that lined the neckline and was trying to decide if she
wanted to put the time into adding the flowers on the
sleeves or to leave them plain. The embroidery was
taking a lot longer than she had thought it would.

Katie's opinion was that it didn't matter. She said
no one would notice the flowers on the sleeves. Sierra,
however, said the little things would matter the most
to Christy on her wedding day. At least, that's how it
had been for Sierra's sister when she got married.

Sierra had come to Christy's dorm room two nights
ago and had arrived just in time to hear Katie's opinion
on the sleeves. A freshman, Sierra was one of the most
free-spirited young women Christy had ever known.
Katie and Christy had met Sierra three years ago, when
they had shared a room in England while on a missions trip.

Sierra's visit to the dorm room had been prompted
by her need to ask if Christy could pick up Sierra from
her job at the local grocery store Friday night.

The last thing Christy needed was to add anything
to her brimming schedule. But she said yes to Sierra

because Christy knew she would have the car since Todd was going on an overnight backpacking trip with some of the guys from the youth group. Even though the trip had been scheduled before Christy and Todd had made their agreement to spend every Saturday together, Todd had offered to cancel the trip. But Christy thought it would be better if he went. She planned to work on wedding plans with Marti and her mom on Saturday.

Marti was back from her extended stay in Wisconsin and had dropped her investigation of the hospital. Apparently, when she had interviewed the surgeon, he told her he had found an inoperable tumor in Grandpa's stomach. Apparently, it had been there for some time and must have bothered him, but he never complained. So by the time it was discovered, it was too late to do anything.

Christy's mom said that Marti had accepted the facts better than any of them had expected. She had dropped the idea of filing charges and had come home ready to dive in to plans for Todd and Christy's wedding. Todd's having asked Bob and Marti to sit on his side in the front row seemed to give Marti even more incentive to be involved.

At the appointed time Friday night, Christy showed up at the grocery store to find Sierra already waiting out front. Sierra was easy to spot because she had long, wild, curly blond hair, and she dressed in unique outfits. Tonight Sierra wore a mid-calf skirt that appeared to be made from neckties sewn together. Her feet were clad in the same pair of cowboy boots she had worn in England when Christy first met her.

"Have you been waiting long?" Christy opened the car door from the inside.

"No, only a few minutes. I finished early because I ran out of sausage."

Christy gave Sierra a strange look. "The grocery store ran out of sausage?"

"No, I did. I was demonstrating. Didn't I tell you that's what I was doing? I go to different grocery stores and hand out samples of whatever the company tells me to. Tonight it was sausages, but they told me only to use twenty packages. I didn't figure out until half-way through that they wanted me to cut the sausages into little pieces and stick toothpicks in them. I was passing out entire sausages, and people were standing there waiting, like I was working at a free hot dog stand."

Christy laughed. "Sounds like a fun job."

"It's perfect for me, except for the transportation. I hate having to bum rides off someone. I really appreciate your doing this for me, Christy."

"No problem. It worked out fine." Her plan was to zip Sierra back to campus and then drive up to her aunt's in Newport Beach since her mom was already there. That way they could start their planning early in the morning.

"Your skirt is adorable," Christy said as she headed out of the parking lot. "Did you make it?"

"My mom helped me. We worked on it over Christmas vacation. I had a short skirt made out of ties, but it got ruined a couple of summers ago. These ties were my grandpa's. Aren't they hilarious? Look at this one."

Sierra pointed to a green-and-brown-striped tie that ran down her left side. It had tiny orange curlicues and thin blue triangles on top of the stripes.

"I guess it would match about anything with all those colors in it," Christy said.

Sierra laughed. "Or not match anything because of all the colors in it. My Granna Mae had a story to tell me about every one of these ties while we were sewing them together. She has serious memory lapses and gets confused and disoriented, but she could remember every minute detail of places she and Grandpa had gone and things they had done when he was wearing these ties."

Christy told Sierra how her grandpa had passed away last month and how much it made her think about the brevity of life.

"I know what you mean," Sierra said. "I've been thinking about that this semester because I've had some big decisions to make."

"By any chance would those decisions be about relationships?" Christy asked.

"Sort of. Are you hungry?" Sierra asked.

"Hungry?"

"Well, The Golden Calf is closed by now, and I've been standing in the grocery store cooking sausages for the past three and a half hours. I could go for something substantial to eat. If you have the time, I'd love to hear your opinion on a few things."

Christy couldn't remember the last time she had hung out with a girl friend for an evening. She could readjust her plans and make the hour and a half drive to Newport Beach early in the morning. After all, she had just made a little speech about the brevity of life. This would be a good time to *carpe* the *diem*.

"Sure," Christy said. "Where should we go?"

"How about The Dove's Nest? Randy and his band are playing there tonight. That's why I couldn't bum a ride from my usual source."

"Okay, it'll be kind of refreshing to see my roommate."

"You and Katie never see each other?" Sierra surmised.

"We're both pretty busy."

"I told my sister that Katie and Rick were getting really close, and she was shocked. Did you know that Rick tried to flirt with Tawni at Doug and Tracy's wedding?"

Christy smiled as she pulled onto the freeway. "I'm not surprised."

"But Katie says he's changed a lot."

"Oh yes, Rick has changed a lot. God has been working in big ways."

"You know what?" Sierra said. "I think Katie and Rick are good for each other. I wouldn't be surprised if they ended up getting married."

"Why do you say that?" Christy asked.

"They're both so vibrant," Sierra said. "The few

times I've seen them together, a sort of electricity flows between them. They spark each other. Katie is energetic all by herself, but when she's with Rick, she's brighter than ever, and so is he. Without her, he's kind of blah."

"That's an interesting way of putting it." Christy had never known anyone to describe Rick as blah. Sierra impressed Christy as someone who didn't let the outward shell of a person distract from the true self, which was hidden within.

They arrived at The Dove's Nest to find the parking lot packed.

"We might not be able to find a place to sit in there," Christy said.

"This is good for Randy and the band," Sierra observed.

"And for Rick."

They entered and spotted a bunch of people they knew from Rancho. Sierra waved at her roommate, Vicki, and Christy said, "Do you want to sit with their group?"

"I'd rather just sit with you so we can talk. Let's see if the couch is open on the bookstore side. Last time I was here people were eating on the couches by the fire."

Christy followed Sierra into the book portion of the store known as The Ark. The fireplace that was open to both the café side and the bookstore side had a couch and two cozy chairs circled around it on The Ark side. The couch was open.

"Perfect!" Christy said. "Would you like to save the couch for us while I order some food?"

Randy's band had just finished a song, and applause rose from the café. Christy was glad they weren't sitting in the noisy café. They could still hear Randy's band from The Ark but could carry on a conversation, as well.

"We could take turns," Sierra suggested. "I don't know what I want."

"Okay." Christy went first, thinking how nice it was to hear someone else say she didn't know what she wanted. That had always been one of Christy's worst problems when ordering at restaurants. She had gotten much better, though.

Tonight she knew she wanted whatever the chef's special was. Katie had been raving about the fabulous chef they recently had hired. Tonight Miguel was offering artichoke pizza with sun-dried tomatoes. It sounded a little unusual, but Christy decided to give it a try. She stepped up to the counter, and Katie noticed her for the first time.

"Chris, when did you get here?"

"Just a few minutes ago. I brought Sierra. Looks like a busy night for you guys."

"Most people are only ordering coffee drinks and desserts, so the kitchen hasn't been swamped. You should try the artichoke pizza. It's really good."

"That's exactly what I wanted. What else do you recommend?"

"I think a small Caesar salad would go nicely with

that," Katie said. "Do you want to try my favorite latte?"

"Sure. We're over on the couch in The Ark."

"I'll bring it to you," Katie said. "What does Sierra want?"

"She's going to place her own order."

Rick stepped up behind Christy and greeted her with a friendly hug. "Did Katie tell you the good news?"

Christy turned to Katie with wide eyes. "No," Christy said. "What good news?"

"Her tea won an honorable mention at the food fair."

"Big whoop," Katie said. "They gave out ten honorable mentions. I'm going to perfect the blend and enter it again next year."

"I thought it was great," Rick said. "Out of thirty-seven entries, she made the top ten. Tell her that's pretty good."

"It really is, Katie," Christy said. "Congratulations."

"Thanks."

"Did Todd come with you?" Rick asked. "I thought he was backpacking this weekend."

"He is. I'm here with Sierra."

"Girls' night out, huh?" Rick turned to Katie. "Have you taken your dinner break yet?"

"No."

"Do you want to take it now?" Rick said. "Dinner is on me, for all three of you."

"Make that two pizzas, Miguel," Katie called out.

"And could you put extra parmesan on mine? Thanks."

"Thanks, Rick," Christy said. "I didn't expect you to pay for us."

"My pleasure. I'd treat you more often, but you never come in."

"I know. This has been the busiest time of my life."

"Todd's too," Rick said. "We never seem to be home at the same time. Sometime the four of us will have to do something together."

"That would be fun," Christy said.

"Hey, tell Todd I was able to work out the deal with the guy my dad knows at the tux shop. It's Burton's Tuxedo Shop. They're in the shopping center down at the stoplight. Next to the video store. I went in today and got measured. All you and Todd have to do is select the style and give him the measurements for the other groomsmen."

"Okay," Christy said slowly.

Katie linked her arm in Christy's. "Come on. I only have an hour."

As they walked away, Christy asked, "Katie, is Rick going to be a groomsman in my wedding?"

"You crack me up, Christy! Of course he is. Todd asked him like three weeks ago. You must be losing it if you can't remember such details."

Christy sat down next to Sierra on the couch and tried hard to remember if Todd had said anything to her. The last Christy had heard, Todd was having his dad for his best man and Doug for his groomsman.

She was having Katie as her maid of honor and Tracy for her bridesmaid. They had agreed weeks ago on only two attendants to keep things simple. The bridesmaids' dresses already were ordered.

Since when did Rick enter the picture?

Christy decided to remain calm and not to get mad at Todd—yet. If he had asked Rick to be in their wedding, he must have had a good reason. Maybe Doug had backed out. Or maybe, since Rick and Todd were sharing an apartment now, he had felt obligated to include Rick in the wedding party.

If Rick is going to be a groomsman along with Doug, then I need another bridesmaid. I wonder if I should ask Sierra now or wait until Todd gets back from his trip.

Katie, Sierra, and Christy sat by the fire and ate while Randy and the band filled the air with original songs that had a wonderfully fresh sound. Christy liked the pizza but told Katie they should have split one because she was full after the salad.

"I'll get doggie bags for us," Katie said. "It'll be just as good in the morning. Breakfast pizza! I'll be right back."

Christy leaned close to Sierra. "We haven't talked about relationships and stuff, like we started to in the car. I didn't know if you wanted to talk privately, or what. We could talk more on the way back to school."

"It's not as if I'm struggling with some huge problem. I just need some input. I'd love to hear what Katie has to say, too."

"Did I hear my name?" Katie asked, returning with a plastic box in her hand.

"I was telling Christy that I could use your advice," Sierra said.

"You came to the right place," Katie said. "It just so happens that my assistant and I are the advice queens. I think Christy is tired of hearing about my life; it'll be refreshing to hear about yours. And since you offered, why don't you start with Paul. What's happening with him?"

"Well, I can summarize that relationship with one of your famous phrases, Katie. Paul and I are 'P.O.'s.' Do you remember the little club we started in England?"

Katie laughed. "Pals Only! I forgot all about that."

"Of course you did," Sierra teased. "You dropped your honorary membership when you started going out with Rick."

"It was unintentional." Katie held up her hand in self-defense. "It was God's idea, not mine. Believe me."

"Oh, I believe you," Sierra said. "It's good to see you guys together, too. It seems natural and like the relationship is alive and growing. It helps me to remember that's how healthy relationships should be."

Christy watched Sierra's face for an indication of what that statement meant. "Did you feel it wasn't going that way for Paul and you?"

Sierra nodded. "How much do you want to hear about Paul?"

"Everything," Katie said.

"Okay," Sierra said. "But you guys asked for it."

Sierra set her tea on the low table in front of the fire and began her story. "You guys know that Paul and I are sort of related now that my sister is married to his brother. Our families were all together at Christmas, and it just became clear to me while we were sitting on the floor watching a video that there's nothing boyfriend-girlfriend between Paul and me. I thought there was for a long time. I hoped there was. I dreamed about what it would be like if there was. And I think both of us gave it a noble effort after he came back from Scotland. But it's not electric."

"Electric?" Katie questioned.

"You know what I mean. I know you know what I mean."

Katie nodded and exchanged glances with Christy.

"Whatever it is that makes a couple realize something deeper and lasting exists between them. Well, I've come to the conclusion Paul and I don't have that . . . whatever it is. We are good, solid friends. He doesn't find me fascinating, and I think he's way too quiet and introspective."

"Have you and Paul talked about this?" Christy asked. "I mean, does he feel the same way?"

"Yes. We went for a long walk at the park the day after Christmas and talked about everything. He started out sounding like he was going to apologize for not being in love with me or something. I stopped him before he said too much and told him how I felt. I told him I was restless, for lack of a better term. I pointed out he was contemplative, which is fine, but it's not a good match for someone like me. He said he felt bad because he had thought something would happen between us, but it just didn't go anywhere. He blamed himself for insisting we take it slow in the beginning and lay a foundation of being good friends.

"I told him that was the best choice because now we are good friends, and I think we'll always be close friends. But that's all."

"You sound like you're okay with that," Christy said.

"I am. I feel free now. I didn't feel free for a long time. I kept thinking there should be something more with Paul. You guys know how much I tortured myself trying to figure out what should happen next with him. I spent months probing my heart, trying to decide how I truly felt about him. It was a long journey that only brought me back to where I started. And that's okay. It's good."

"If I've learned one thing," Katie said, sipping her

latte and looking settled in her own understanding, "it's that God writes a different story for each of our lives. Sometimes you think you know what's going to happen, but then the plot takes an unexpected turn."

"And sometimes you have to end one chapter before you can start the next," Sierra said. "I have so many dreams, you guys. I want to travel. I want to be free to go wherever I want to go for the next season of my life. I've already signed up for an education extension program that Rancho offers. And guess where it's held?"

"Where?" Katie asked.

"Brazil! Doesn't that sound like a fun place to go?"

"Sounds like you're going to become a world traveler," Christy said.

"It started with that trip to England, when I met you guys. Then, Christy, you invited me to Switzerland with you and your aunt. I got the bug. I love traveling."

Christy could picture Sierra trekking around the globe in her cowboy boots. She definitely had an adventuresome spirit.

"When I started college last semester, it was strange. I had been so excited to come to Rancho. But then, there I was, sitting in classes, and all I could think about was getting out of there and traveling. I kept running into people on campus who had been to exotic places. I would tell myself I should concentrate on finishing my freshman year and getting serious about Paul. I thought I should try to arrange a normal life, like my sister and the rest of my friends have. But you know what? It didn't fit. I never felt at peace. After Paul and I had our talk at Christmas, I felt free. That's the only way I can explain it. Nothing is holding me back. It's like you said, Katie, God is writing my life story, and it's different for me than it is for anyone else."

"You're right, Sierra," Christy said. "God is going to make your path clear."

"More than that," Katie added. " 'God will fulfill his purpose for you.' That's a promise. Psalm 138. Verse 8."

Sierra sipped the last of her tea and nodded. "You know what, you guys? This is the first time I've sat down to explain my feelings as one complete thought. When I listen to myself talking to you like this, it makes sense. It doesn't sound as if I'm cutting my strings and flying off like a kite."

Christy gave Sierra a comforting smile. "And what if you are cutting your strings? If God created you to be a kite, then the only right answer for you, the only obedient response, would be to go fly—be free. It shouldn't matter if other people understand. You're the one who knows in your heart of hearts when you're obeying His direction. He's the One who will lift you up and send you soaring."

"Thank you so much, Christy. I needed to hear that." In a less-than-graceful gesture, Sierra reached over and hugged Christy around the neck. Then Sierra hugged Katie. "You two are amazing."

Christy noticed some movement out of the corner

of her eye that made her hold her breath. Rick had positioned himself a few feet away. His gaze was fixed on Katie, and he seemed to be enchanted with her.

A happy, settled feeling came over Christy's heart. *Go ahead, Rick Doyle, admire Katie all you want. She's amazing, isn't she? And so are you. I have absolutely no doubt the Lord will fulfill His purpose for the two of you.*

Early the next morning, Christy stopped by the campus coffee shop for a cup of coffee to drink on the way to Aunt Marti's. She picked up her mail from her campus mailbox and found a card from her grandma. Reading as she walked back to the car, Christy checked the last few lines twice since they didn't immediately make sense to her. Her grandmother had thanked Christy and Todd for coming to the funeral. Then she wrote,

Christina, I was surprised to see how much you have grown to resemble Martha with your way of keeping on top of things. Make sure you leave room in your life for peace. I'm sure Todd will encourage you in this area.

Christy thought her grandmother must have gotten confused when she said Christy resembled Aunt Marti. *No way am I like Aunt Marti. Grandma must have meant Margaret, my mom, but she wrote "Martha." I hope Grandma isn't experiencing memory failure the way Sierra's Granna Mae is.*

It took Christy an hour and forty-five minutes to drive to Newport Beach. When she arrived, Margaret and Martha, the two sisters, were standing in the kitchen, peering at a book on the counter and having a good laugh. Christy noticed the list Marti had printed out, waiting for them on the counter.

"What's so funny?" Christy asked.

"It's more of those cakes that are designed for each couple based on how they met," Mom said, pointing to a picture on the counter. This cake was in the shape of a horse's head. The statue of the bride and groom was stuck in the icing between the horse's ears.

"Let me guess," Christy said. "They met at a horse race."

"No, a riding stable. They've been horsing around ever since!" Marti said gleefully.

Christy shook her head at her aunt's attempt at a joke. Marti's delight in her role as wedding "director" affirmed to Christy that Todd was right about delegating more details to Marti.

"I hope this isn't our only choice of bakeries." Christy turned the next few pages. "I would prefer a simple white wedding cake. And definitely without the plastic bride and groom."

Mom turned to Marti. "I told you Christy would know what she wanted. Once she's organized, she knows exactly what she wants."

"I understand that," Marti said. "That's why I said I wanted to help her get organized. I hope you brought your list so we can compare notes, Christy."

Christy nodded. *Was my grandmother right? Am I more like my aunt than I realized?*

"Where's Uncle Bob this morning?" Christy asked.

"He had a men's breakfast at church," Marti said.

Christy noticed Aunt Marti didn't sound disgusted about Bob's involvement in church the way she used to. That was a good sign that her heart was softening. At least, Christy hoped it was softening.

"You didn't want him here today to help make decisions, did you?" Marti said. "These details are beyond him. Whatever we decide, he'll be happy."

Mom smiled at Christy. "That sounds like someone else we know."

"Todd," Christy said flatly.

Todd is just like Uncle Bob. I'm like Marti. Opposites attract. But I can't be like Aunt Marti! I don't want to spend my life micromanaging everyone around me!

Christy pulled up a stool at the kitchen counter and sat down. *This is a terrible revelation. I've become my aunt!*

"I only kept these pictures to show you for fun," Marti said, placing them to the side. "Of course, I understand you want a more traditional cake. I have those pictures right here."

What was it my grandmother said about making room for peace? That's what I need to do. I have to learn to be at peace with myself and with people around me. That's what's missing from my aunt's life. She doesn't have peace.

Christy silently prayed as Marti showed her pictures of traditional wedding cakes. A peculiar peace came over Christy. It was the reaffirming sense that God had created her to be the way she was for a reason. Wasn't that what she had told Sierra last night? It was time to take her own advice and to become her own person.

No, that's not right. That's what my aunt used to say to me when I was a teenager. She said I needed to be my own person and to my own self be true. But that doesn't bring peace. The only right way to live my life is to be God's person. To fully become the woman God created me to be, tidiness issues and all. There's nothing wrong with being organized and, as my grandma said, "on top of things." As long as I don't run ahead of God and others. What matters is whether I live a life at peace with God. That's the only way I'll be at peace with myself and with others.

Christy leaned back from the kitchen counter and drew in a deep, wobbly breath.

"Are you okay?" Mom turned away from the cake pictures to look at Christy.

A smile started in the secret corner of Christy's heart and scooted all the way to her face, where it broke through with all its radiant, peace-filled implications.

"More than okay," Christy said. "I think I might be better than I've ever been. I'm not a kite like Sierra. But now I know how to go fly—be free. In here," she said, patting her heart. "I think I finally understand who I am."

"Whatever are you rambling about?" Marti scrutinized Christy's big smile.

14 "Nothing," Christy said and then quickly corrected herself. "Actually, it's everything. It's God. He just showed me something, and I understand myself more clearly than ever."

Both Mom and Marti looked at her.

Christy giggled. "It's okay. I can tell you about it later. Go ahead, Aunt Marti. What were you saying about this cake?"

Marti cleared her throat. She seemed a bit uncomfortable that God had interrupted her presentation to have a counseling session with Christy.

It's okay, Aunt Marti. I understand your frustration more than I ever have before. Todd was right. The Bridegroom is here. And He will show up at our wedding no matter what kind of cake we have. But we can plan the cake and everything else and still live in peace. We just have to let God be in control, not us.

"I was saying, what do you think of lemon cake instead of white? They use a marvelous almond filling instead of that pasty white frosting." With that, Marti went full speed ahead with her collected information on wedding cakes. She had two cake samples for Christy and her mom to try that she had picked up while interviewing pastry chefs that week.

Christy liked the one with the raspberry filling the best. Marti questioned Christy twice before making a note of Christy's choice.

Without a moment's hesitation, Marti moved on to the flowers, presenting Christy with at least fifty pictures of possible bouquets.

"I'd like white carnations," Christy said when she looked at the first picture.

Marti ignored her and turned to a gigantic bouquet of red roses laced with baby's breath.

"I'd like white carnations," Christy said again after they had gone through half of the pictures. "White carnations with some baby's breath would be just fine."

Marti nodded and moved right on to the next stack of pictures, pointing out an exotic bouquet with miniature white roses and large white gardenias.

Christy said again, "I'd like white carnations."

"Christy, darling, white carnations are so plain."

Christy's mom stepped in. "Todd's first bouquet for her was white carnations."

"I know that," Marti snapped. "I was there. But this isn't a high school date to the prom. This is their wedding. Why not consider a variety of flowers, such as this bouquet?" She pointed to a mixture of purple, blue, and yellow flowers in a sweet, small bouquet.

Suddenly Christy had an idea. "What about this? I would really love this bouquet, but not with all the bright colors. Could you have the florist make a bouquet of all white flowers?"

"Of course," Marti said.

"I'd like it to have white carnations, baby's breath, those tiny white roses, some gardenias, and white plumeria."

"Now, that sounds like an elegant assortment." Marti reached for her pen to write it all down.

"But I don't want it to be huge like some of these. I want a small, happy, little bouquet."

"Wedding bouquets are supposed to be dramatic," Marti said. "The bouquet is used to complete the gown and veil and pull it all together in one focal point."

"My gown isn't going to be dramatic. It's simple. I think my bouquet should be simple, too."

"And what about your veil?" Marti asked.

Christy glanced at her mom. "We haven't decided on that yet. I know I want a sheer veil that hangs over my face, but I don't know what I want to use as the headpiece."

"A hat, perhaps?"

"No."

"I've got it!" Marti flipped through a stack of magazines she hadn't presented to Christy yet. "You would look adorable in one of these wreaths." She pulled out a Hawaiian magazine and pointed to the girl on the cover. "The flowers are fixed in a wreath that you wear on your head like a crown. You could place the wreath over the veil."

"I love it!" Christy exclaimed.

"You do?" Marti looked shocked that one of her ideas was received on the first pitch.

"Yes! Todd wanted me to wear flowers in my hair. That would be perfect. I'd want it to be all white flowers and narrower than the one shown here. Oh, Aunt Marti, what a perfect suggestion!"

Marti leaned against the counter and tilted her head as she examined Christy. "I believe that is the first time I've made a suggestion you've been enthusiastic about."

"That's because it's a great idea! It's perfect, don't you think, Mom?"

Mom looked a little more serious. "I'm wondering how difficult it would be to find a florist who can do something like that and make it turn out right."

"That's not a problem," Marti said. "Bob knows a florist on Maui. We'll have him make it and ship it to arrive the next day so the flowers will still be fresh and carry that irresistible island fragrance. You know, Christy, you really must use tuberose."

"Are those the little white flowers they use to make leis? The ones that smell so good?"

"Yes. And they're small. Much smaller than the plumeria. You might have trouble with the plumeria staying fresh. They turn brown when they're touched a lot, you know."

Christy felt her heart swelling with glee. Her bouquet was going to be gorgeous, and this was the perfect solution to her veil. Todd would love that she was wearing Hawaiian flowers in her hair. Christy knew she would have a hard time not telling Todd what her complete outfit was going to look like. But she knew she must keep it a secret; he would have to wait and be surprised when he saw her. She had a feeling he would be more than surprised. Todd would be amazed as only a man in love can be, a man who has waited for the day when he would see his bride dressed all in white from her heart to her toes coming down the aisle toward him.

Christy's mom continued to study the pictures on the counter. "The small white flowers in your wreath will go nicely with the flowers you're embroidering on your dress."

"What dress is she embroidering?" Marti asked.

"Her wedding dress," Mom said. "Or perhaps I should say my wedding dress."

"Our wedding dress." Christy gave her mom a warm smile. "Would you like to see it, Aunt Marti?"

"Why didn't I know about this?" Marti asked. "I was under the impression you hadn't made a decision on your gown."

"No, we have the wedding gown all figured out." Christy pulled the bodice from her overnight bag and held it up for her aunt and Mom to see. She had decided to leave the sleeves plain and was happy now with that choice because the emphasis was on the bodice's delicate flowers.

"You embroidered this?" Marti examined the careful stitches in the delicate string of forget-me-nots. "Why, Christina, it's exquisite."

"Thank you."

"This was from your dress, Margaret?"

"Yes. You did a beautiful job on this, Christy. I brought the skirt, and I'm ready to baste it to the bodice whenever you're ready for a fitting."

"I'm ready," Christy said. "Oh, and did you bring the addresses for the invitations, Mom?"

"Yes, I brought them."

"Good, because I picked up the invitations this week. They only took two weeks to print, which was sooner than they said it would be when Todd and I ordered them."

"Wonderful," Marti said. "I'll take them over to Fiona's this week, and she can start the calligraphy right away."

"What else do we need to decide on?" Christy asked.

Marti went through her list. They had an appointment with the photographer in an hour, and if they wanted to go to the bakery after that, they could taste the other cake flavors, in case Christy wanted to change her mind on the lemon cake with raspberry filling.

"No, I'm sure I want the raspberry." She knew her

aunt preferred the almond filling. "Todd loves fruit, Aunt Marti. I hate nuts, so raspberry is the best choice for us."

"All right. Fine."

Christy felt at peace. This was going well.

"The last item we need to go over is the catering service for the reception." Marti had a lot of information for them to go over and suggested they wait until the afternoon.

"Okay," Christy agreed.

"I think this would be a good time for me to bring in the skirt to your dress," Mom said. She left Christy and Marti alone in the kitchen.

Christy took the opportunity to give her aunt a big hug and a kiss on the cheek.

"What was that for?"

"For being here," Christy said.

"Well, of course I'm here." Marti brushed off the comment as if she had caught Christy's deeper meaning but didn't want to acknowledge it.

Christy chose to press the point. "You could have been in Santa Fe right now making pottery at The Colony. Last fall, you told me that's what you intended to do. I'm so glad you stayed. I'm glad you kept your promise to Uncle Bob."

Marti bristled. "What promise?"

"To love, honor, and cherish him for better or worse, in sickness and in health, for richer or for poorer, until death do you part."

"I see you're practicing your wedding vows. Sounds

like you have them nicely memorized." Marti straightened the pictures and lists on the counter. She wouldn't look at Christy.

"And you're practicing them, too, with your life," Christy said. "I love you, Aunt Marti. I want you to know that I appreciate your helping me by doing what you do best, lining up everything. You are the perfect wedding coordinator. More than that, I'm glad you're here for my wedding. I'm glad you're not in Santa Fe."

Marti glanced at Christy and then looked away. "It's not easy. You'll find out soon enough. Life doesn't always go the way you think it will."

"The Lord will fulfill His purpose for you, Aunt Marti." Christy hadn't expected to say that. It just tumbled out. But her heart was filled with peace, and she longed for her aunt to know that same peace.

How can I tell her in a way she'll understand? Lord, what do you want my aunt to hear?

"I know the Lord will fulfill His purpose for you," Christy repeated. "But you have to trust Him with all your heart and surrender your life to Him."

Marti drew in a deep breath without taking her eyes off the coffee mug that sat on the counter in front of her. With slow, careful words she said, "I have been considering that, Christina."

Christy's heart pounded wildly. She had waited for years to hear her aunt say she was opening her heart even just a sliver. When Marti didn't add any further comments, Christy leaned over and spoke softly, giving her aunt the image that was so clear in Christy's mind at that moment. "Can I tell you some thoughts I've been having lately about weddings?"

"Of course," Marti said. "That's what we're focusing on today, isn't it?"

"These thoughts are about heaven and how the Bible talks about Christ being the groom."

Marti turned her dark, solemn eyes toward Christy.

"I don't know if you've ever heard it explained like this, but in a way, Christ has proposed to each of us and asked us to be His bride so that we can be with Him. Forever."

Since Marti wasn't stopping her, Christy went on. "We can't come to God as we are because of our sin. He's pure and holy, and we're not. That's why God allowed His only Son to die in our place. Jesus paid the price for our disobedience. But you already know all that, Aunt Marti. You know that God wants us to be made clean so that nothing would separate us from Him."

Christy swallowed her rising emotions. "I don't know if you know this, but He wants to give you a new heart, Aunt Marti. God wants you to take His salvation like a wedding dress. It's a pure, white, immensely expensive wedding dress. It cost Him His life. He offers it to all of us to wear as we walk this long aisle of life. But we have to put on His gift."

Christy realized she was using her hands to demonstrate the act of taking off the old and putting on the new, pure, white gown offered by God. She tucked her hands behind her back and concluded her thought. "Then, when we reach the end of the long aisle of life, we will stand before Christ. He is the true Bridegroom. He loves us with all His heart and has been waiting for us to come to Him since the day we were born."

Marti didn't take her eyes off Christy. Tiny wrinkles began to crease her smooth forehead. Tears glistened in the corners of her eyes. "You believe this, don't you, Christina?"

"Yes, with all my heart."

Marti pressed her lips together as if she were commanding her words to stay locked inside.

Christy couldn't believe how clearly she had communicated the message she had wanted to give to her aunt for years. She hadn't planned the words or the imagery; it was simply there. Todd was the one who always had the great analogies.

Maybe Todd's way of seeing things is beginning to rub off on me. Or maybe the more I trust God, the more He can use me just the way I am to speak the truth in love.

Marti reached over and covered Christy's hand with hers. Christy noticed how cold and moist Marti's hand felt. In a low voice, she said, "Don't give up on me, Christina. I am very close."

Just as Christy's mom was about to enter the kitchen, Marti let go of Christy's hand.

Christy leaned closer to her aunt. "I won't give up on you, Aunt Marti. And neither will God. He is the relentless lover, and you are His first love. He won't give up because He wants you back."

Marti turned to walk away. "I need to put on some lipstick, and then we must leave for our appointment with the photographer."

"Is she okay?" Mom asked as Marti disappeared.

Christy's face was lit up with a huge smile as she nodded. "More than okay. She's great."

"Do you want to have a quick look at this?"

Mom pulled the bag off the skirt to the wedding gown, and Christy released a long "Oooh."

"I think it turned out real nice, don't you?"

"Mom, it's perfect. I love the way the folds add full-ness without making it poof out." Christy held up the bodice to the skirt. "It's going to be beautiful. Thank you so much, Mom! I love it."

"Very nice," Marti concurred when she reappeared. She seemed unaffected by the intimate conversation she and Christy had just shared. "It's simple and sweet. Just like you. Have you given any thought to what undergarments would work best with that, Christy? I think we should add lingerie shopping to our list for this afternoon."

Christy had done plenty of shopping with her aunt over the years. Lingerie shopping wasn't something they had attempted yet, and Christy wasn't sure how she felt about shopping with her mom and aunt for fancy underwear.

"But first we must get to the photographer's." Marti scurried them to the door.

They met with the professional photographer, looked through dozens of albums, and selected a plan that they all seemed happy with. Christy thought the photo package was outrageously expensive, but Marti said it was one of the parts of the wedding she and Uncle Bob were covering, so Christy shouldn't worry her pretty little head about it.

"What matters is that you hire a quality professional who captures the look you want," Marti said.

Christy thought of the picture she had seen of her parents' wedding on the hallway wall at her grandmother's. She doubted if a professional who charged extravagant fees had taken the picture. Yet the photo captured the mood of the day and the delight of the parents and happy couple.

"I'd also like to have a bunch of instant cameras on all the tables at the reception," Christy said. "That way the guests can snap pictures of each other, and we'll have a lot of candid shots for our scrapbook."

"We can do that," Marti said as she drove down Pacific Coast Highway on her way to a restaurant she wanted them to try. She explained that the chef was available for catering weddings.

Christy suggested the chef at The Dove's Nest, but Marti shrugged off the idea. Then Christy reminded her aunt that the reception was being held at Rancho Corona, and it made more sense to have a caterer located close to the school. Marti said that caterers were used to traveling all over southern California, and the location didn't matter.

Christy dropped the subject. It wasn't worth arguing over now, after they had peacefully agreed on so many other topics that day. She also felt a new sense of responsibility toward her aunt. Marti had willingly listened as Christy presented the Gospel to her that morning with the wedding analogy. Christy didn't want to invalidate any of that by being disagreeable with her aunt, who was doing so much to help with the wedding.

At the end of their full day, Christy decided to spend the night at Bob and Marti's and go to church with her uncle in the morning. She called Todd to tell him she wouldn't see him until she returned to her dorm room Sunday afternoon. She only got the voice mail again. She missed Todd. It would be so nice to feel his arms around her and to tell him about their cake having raspberry filling and the details of the photographer's wedding package.

She wouldn't tell him about the flowers or her veil. Or the beautiful assortment of lingerie Marti and her mom had bought for her that afternoon. Those would all be surprises.

Todd didn't call on Sunday after she returned to her dorm, but that didn't surprise her. He probably was exhausted after the backpacking trip and had a lot of work to do at the church sorting out the gear and putting things away.

While they had been shopping on Saturday, Marti had asked Christy if she had any idea what she would buy Todd as a wedding gift. Marti insisted the bride and groom traditionally gave each other gifts. The first thing that popped out of Christy's mouth was, "I'm giving Todd a cell phone so he won't be so hard to get ahold of." She had said it as a joke, but now it was beginning to seem like a good idea. They could get matching his-and-her phones.

Katie meandered into their dorm room at seven o'clock that evening with another bright bouquet of mixed flowers and a plastic pitcher full of water.

"He loves me," Katie said simply.

Christy smiled. "Did Rick tell you he loved you?"

"No, he just keeps showing me that he does. I was a grump all weekend because I'm so behind on schoolwork. I haven't finished my economics paper yet; so instead of playing raquetball like we had planned, Rick and I spent the afternoon at the library gathering all the info and statistics. Then he gave me these flowers and thanked me for a wonderful day."

Katie adjusted the flowers in the plastic vase. She seemed serene and dreamy in her relationship with Rick. That settledness was in sharp contrast to the way she had flown into their room on a caffeine high several months ago and asked Christy if it might be possible Katie was in love.

"You know what? I have a feeling this guy isn't going to give up on me." The tone of Katie's voice reminded Christy of her aunt when she had asked Christy not to give up on her. The comparison between a forever love relationship with God and a bride and groom making a commitment to each other seemed stronger than ever to Christy.

That's how it is with relentless lovers, Christy thought. *They don't give up, do they? In the same way Rick is wooing you, Katie, Jesus has been wooing Aunt Marti. And I don't think either of them is going to give up. Ever.*

With her flowers perfectly arranged on her desk, Katie stretched out on what she called the surfin' sofa. "So how was your weekend, Christy? Did you make a lot of plans at Marti's?"

Christy excitedly gave Katie a rundown of all the details. She told Katie about her aunt's receptiveness as Christy talked with her about the Lord. She also told Katie about the flowers and the head wreath and how the flowers were going to come from Maui. Then she pulled two boxes out from under her bed and showed Katie her beautiful new lingerie.

"I've never owned anything like this," Christy said. "I love it. And it actually was fun shopping for it with my mom and my aunt. It made me feel like one of the girls, if that makes sense."

"What about the doctor?" Katie asked.

"What doctor?"

"Have you made an appointment yet with a gynecologist to get checked out?"

"No, I need to do that. It's on my list. I'm going to the same one my mom goes to in Escondido. She gave me the number a few weeks ago. I just haven't called yet."

"How do you feel about all that?" Katie lowered her voice. "The honeymoon, I mean. Are you ready for, you know . . . everything."

Christy felt like shouting, "Yes! Yes! A thousand times yes!" But she nodded calmly and simply said, "Yes, I'm ready."

"Do you guys want to have kids right away?" Katie asked.

Christy realized that even though they had talked about how many children they wanted and about giving them Hawaiian middle names, they hadn't discussed the specifics of when.

"We're still talking that through," Christy said.

"Have you and Todd had any huge arguments?"

Christy wasn't sure where Katie was coming up with these random questions. "Yes, of course."

"Rick and I had a huge fight yesterday. It took us about an hour and a half to talk it through and come to an agreement. I think it was good for both of us, though. I mean, if Rick wanted to walk away after seeing me at my worst, that would have been the moment. If he was going to give up on me, it probably would have been yesterday."

"Sounds like your relationship is getting pretty real," Christy said.

"Yes, it is. It's getting real." Katie looked at Christy

and then gave her short red hair a little flip. "And I think I like it that way."

On Monday afternoon Todd called Christy at the campus bookstore where she was working. "Hey, what are you doing tonight?" he asked.

She had to smile. They hadn't spoken in three days since he had left on the backpack trip. Still, he didn't start their conversation with a normal "Hi, how are you." Although Todd never had started phone conversations with "Hi, how are you." For a while it was, "Hey, how's it going?" Now it was just a leap right to the point.

Christy decided to answer him with the same forthrightness he had asked the question. "Homework."

"Homework, huh? What's that?"

"Oh, be nice!" Christy turned away from the cash register since she didn't have any customers at the moment. "Have you already forgotten what it's like for the rest of us who aren't yet college graduates?"

"Yes." Lowering his voice, he added, "I miss you, Kilikina."

"I miss you more," she countered.

"Not possible," he said. "Hey, do you think you can ignore your homework for one night and go out to dinner with me?"

"You tell me when and where, and I'll be there."

"Don't laugh," Todd said. "But I'd like to go to The Golden Calf and eat at our table by the window. I miss meeting you there."

"Okay, what time?"

"Five-fifteen if you want me in my painting clothes. Six o'clock if you want me clean."

"I'll take 5:15," Christy said.

Eager to make sure no one snatched their table, Christy left the bookstore immediately when she got off at five. She went directly to their table and waited only a few minutes before she spotted Todd coming toward her. It was all she could do not to jump up, dash across the cafeteria, and throw her arms around her beloved. He was wearing his grungy paint clothes and a smile on his face broad enough and bright enough to start a small forest fire.

One thing was certain. His presence lit a blazing fire in the hearth of her soul. She rose to greet him with a kiss and a tight hug.

"Good thing this paint is dry," Todd said.

Christy pulled away and checked her clothes. Todd was right. His speckled work clothes hadn't transferred any paint onto her.

"Have you already eaten?" Todd asked.

"No, I came a little early to wait for you."

"I'll get your food for you," he offered. "What would you like?"

"Anything. I'm not even hungry. I just want to talk with you."

"We have a lot to talk about, don't we. I'll be right back."

Christy watched Todd move through the line, greeting friends and getting their food. She thought again about the similarities between having a relationship with the Lord and falling in love. The parallels seemed to be everywhere, now that she was watching for them.

What would my relationship with the Lord be like if I set a time to meet with Him every day? Would I show up early just because I couldn't wait to talk with Him?

After Todd returned to the table, Christy said she wanted to pray for them before they ate. With a full heart, she thanked God for Todd and for the chance to be together during their busy week. She told Jesus she wanted to grow more in love with Him so that she would find a fire lit in the hearth of her soul every day and that she would meet with Him there with an open heart.

"Amen!" Todd said.

"As you wish," she said to conclude the prayer. Looking up, she smiled at Todd.

He smiled back.

"I wish I had understood love sooner," Christy said. "I wish I had known when I was younger what it meant to be in love like this. If I had, I think my relationship with the Lord would be so much deeper than it is now. I just didn't understand."

Todd nodded. "Hey, I talked to your uncle today, and he said Marti is really opening up to the Lord. He said you had a talk with her on Saturday that she told him about."

Christy gave Todd a summary of what had gone on all weekend. He told her about the backpacking trip.

She told him about going to The Dove's Nest on Friday with Sierra and that reminded her of Rick's message about the tux shop.

"I thought I told you I was going to ask Rick to be one of the groomsmen," Todd said.

"No, I think I would have remembered if you had. It means we now have three groomsmen and only two bridesmaids."

"Four." Todd speared a piece of broccoli with his fork. "Doug, my dad, Rick, and David."

"David? My brother? When did you ask David to be a groomsman?"

"A couple of weeks ago. I know we talked about that one."

"I remember us talking about whether or not we wanted to have a candlelighter, and how David could do that."

"Right," Todd said.

"But then we decided we didn't want a candle-lighter because we were getting married outside," Christy said.

"Right. So I asked David to be a groomsman. He was pretty happy about it. I think he'll feel like he's included in the wedding more, don't you?"

So that was Todd's logic. That was the way his mind worked. Deep down, he was considering the welfare of others. David would feel included. That was important to Todd.

Christy knew then that for the rest of her life, no matter how organized she would be, the unpredictable factor of Todd's logic would always come into play.

For the next ten minutes, they discussed what Christy labeled the "random factor." She knew this quality of Todd's would be with them on the long journey ahead, and she was determined to make peace with it. She gave Todd examples of when it already had affected their relationship, such as when he stopped under the freeway in Carlsbad to share his breakfast with the homeless man. Todd didn't see his pattern of thinking as anything unusual, but he said he would try to remember to run decisions past Christy before he acted on them.

"So, do you think you can live with it?" Todd asked. "Me, I mean. My logic. This 'random factor.' Will I drive you crazy?"

"Probably," Christy said with a grin. "No more than I'll drive you crazy with my tidiness issues."

"I think we're getting better at this, don't you? We're learning how to keep each other balanced." Todd returned her wide smile.

Christy noticed he had tiny flecks of beige paint across his forehead and a small piece of broccoli stuck between his front two teeth.

Okay, this is starting to get pretty real here!

Christy motioned to Todd he had something in his teeth and remembered one of their earliest dates. They had taken Uncle Bob's tandem bike to Balboa Island, and Todd had bought her an ice cream dipped in chocolate. On the bike ride back, the chocolate had somehow smeared across her face, but Todd hadn't said anything to her, even though she found out after he left that she looked ridiculous.

It wouldn't be like that now. We've come a long way in our relationship. Todd would tell me if I had chocolate on my face. Or broccoli in my teeth. We're a team. A good team. We balance each other, just like he said.

"Did I tell you about the trip to Mexico this weekend?" Todd asked.

"What trip to Mexico?"

"Several of the men from church want to go down to work on the orphanage. They plan to leave Thursday night and come back Saturday night. Do you want to go with us?"

Christy tried to remember what she had just told herself about their being a good team, but the thoughts escaped her. "Todd, I'm swamped this weekend. I have classes Friday, and I work until six. There's no way I can change things around to go to Mexico with you!"

Then, because she knew she needed to express everything she was thinking, she tried in a kind way to say, "You realize, don't you, that you're leaving for the second weekend in a row?"

"I know. That's why I hoped you could come with us. I can get out of it, I think."

"It sounds like you should go," Christy said.

"What about us? What about our wedding plans?"

"I can work on everything. We have . . . what? Seven or eight more weekends after this one."

"I'll make sure I don't schedule myself for anything

during the next eight weekends," Todd said.

Christy leaned forward. "Just promise me you won't schedule anything for the weekend of May twenty-second. That weekend definitely is booked."

"Got it on my calendar."

Christy looked at him skeptically. "Do you even own a calendar?"

Todd shrugged. "No, just the one on the back of my checkbook. But I circled May twenty-second on that calendar."

Christy laughed. A few months ago she might have cried; now she laughed.

Todd watched her laugh with a settled look on his face. "Why did I think we could pull this off in January?"

Christy laughed more. "Sometimes I wish we *had* pulled it off in January. We would be married now."

"But a rushed wedding wouldn't have been as special as the one you're making for us," Todd said.

"Do you want to talk about a few of the wedding details?" Christy asked. "It would be good for us to make a couple of decisions tonight, especially since you're going to be gone this weekend."

"Sure. Like what?"

"Tuxes."

"Okay, let's go look at tuxes."

"Now?" Christy asked.

"Sure, why not?"

"Why not?" Christy echoed.

With a few more quick bites of dinner, Todd and

Christy left the cafeteria, jumped into their Volvo, and drove down the hill to Burton's Tuxedo Shop. Todd hummed as he drove.

Christy reached over and gave his arm three squeezes. "Hey, you're getting pretty muscular there."

Todd raised his eyebrows. "Never underestimate the power of moving a paintbrush up and down a wall all day."

Christy grinned and gave his arm another squeeze. He flexed and she laughed, remembering how her dad used to invite Christy and David to each grab on to his arm muscles when they were little. Her dad would then flex both arm muscles like a strong man and lift them off the ground.

"You're my hero," Christy said sweetly.

Now Todd laughed. "Need any bars of steel bent? Any tall buildings you want me to leap over?"

"No," Christy said firmly. "Just stand still and let the guy measure you when we get to this tux shop."

"Got it." Todd went back to humming a song Christy didn't recognize.

"What is that? I've heard you hum it before."

"It's a song I've been working on. I'll sing it for you sometime."

"Sing it now," Christy said.

Todd flashed her a big smile. "Naw, it's better with the guitar. Just wait. I'll sing it for you one day. I promise."

They entered Burton's Tuxedo Shop hand in hand with Todd still humming. The man who stood behind the counter seemed reluctant to take them seriously. Christy guessed it was because of how Todd looked. They sat down and began to look through the book of selected styles.

On the fifth page, Todd said, "That's it. That's the one. What do you think, Christy?"

She thought she would like to look at the rest of the pages and then go back and look at them again before deciding.

"It's nice. It's basic. The classic tux," Todd said. "I think this is the one. What do you think?"

"It's nice."

"So we can go with this one?"

"Sure." Christy hadn't seen anything she particularly liked on the preceding pages, and she reminded herself Todd would be the one wearing the tux, after all. He should be the one to decide what he wanted to wear.

"Sir?" Todd called across the room. "Would you mark the Spencer-Miller party down for five of these?"

Christy covered her mouth with her hand. Having just gone through several formal meetings over the weekend with her mom and aunt, Christy thought Todd's way of handling things was atrocious. He sounded as if he were ordering five tacos to go.

"It's five, right?" Todd asked.

Christy uncovered her mouth. "Six. My dad decided to wear a tux after all. I don't know if Uncle Bob wants to wear the same style."

"Sir?" Todd hollered to the man behind the

counter. "Could you make that seven?"

"Todd, why don't we just go over there and talk to him," Christy suggested.

They filled out the paper work. Todd put down a deposit. Then the store clerk asked Todd to stand in front of the mirrors so he could be measured. Todd stretched out his arms and fortunately kept his comments to a minimum.

Within ten minutes the process was complete, and they were back on the road to school. Christy wondered if some of Todd's carefree approach to life would rub off on her after they were married.

Until that happened, she still had some less-than-carefree topics to discuss with him, starting with the wedding party. They stopped at an ice-cream shop on their way back to campus and ate at a corner table.

Todd didn't seem to grasp the problem of having four groomsmen while Christy only had two attendants. "I don't think it should matter if the sides are uneven."

"It matters to me," Christy said. "I should ask two other friends to stand with me." She thought about whom she would ask. It had been so simple when it was just Katie and Tracy. Neither she nor Todd had any sisters or close cousins to include.

"I could ask Doug and Rick just to be ushers. They wouldn't have to stand with me," Todd said.

"No, I don't think the answer is to uninvite any of the men. It would be better if I chose two more women. The only problem is I don't really have any other friends I'm especially close to, or at least close enough to ask them to be in our wedding. Sierra is the only one I can think of, and I wouldn't feel right asking her now. She would know she was an afterthought."

Christy had always been a one-best-friend kind of person. Paula had been that best friend all the way through elementary and junior high. The two of them always said they would be each other's bridesmaids; however, they had grown apart when Christy moved to California. Last summer Paula got married, and Christy received an invitation but wasn't able to attend.

Then she realized how much her year in Switzerland had chopped up her relationships. She had friends in Europe, but it was unlikely any of them could come to the wedding. Her first few years of college she had lived at home and attended a community college. She hadn't developed any lasting friendships there. Her list of friends suddenly seemed very short.

"Why don't we mix the men and women on both sides?" Todd suggested. "I mean, it's our wedding, right? We can do whatever we want. We could have my dad, Doug, and Tracy on my side, and then Katie, Rick, and David on your side."

Christy contemplated Todd's suggestion. Once again, his unique way of looking at things opened a world of possibilities to her.

"What do you think?" Todd asked.

Christy had to smile, remembering when he had asked her that question as they shopped for engagement rings. With a big grin, Christy said, "What do I think? I think you kiss pretty good."

Todd seemed to appreciate her humor. He responded with one of her lines. "Do you want to talk mushy or business? I was asking about the wedding attendants."

With a playful grin Christy said, "Mushy, of course. But I'll try to refrain myself and stick to business by saying that once again your clever random factor has saved the day by coming up with an unexpected solution to a problem that had my tidiness issues and me in a panic."

Todd laughed, scooped up her empty ice-cream cup, and carried it to the trash can at the other end of the ice-cream shop.

Just then Christy noticed some students from Rancho coming in the door. Sierra was with them. Christy waved at her, and Sierra left her group to come over to talk to Christy.

Sierra sat down in Todd's empty chair. "I'm glad you're here. I wanted to ask, when is your wedding date?"

"May twenty-second."

"Good! I was hoping that was the day. I was accepted for the summer study program I told you about. My flight leaves the next Saturday. I didn't want to miss your wedding."

"Oh good. I'm glad you'll be there," Christy said.

"Me too. I've also been meaning to thank you." Sierra bent her head toward Christy.

Christy noticed Todd was talking with the students who had come in with Sierra. She gave Sierra her full attention.

"What you said to me at The Nest about being who God made me to be has really helped. Especially as I've prepared for this trip to Brazil."

"In a way, it helped me, too." Christy was thinking about how she had discovered she was a lot like her aunt but how that had turned out to be a good thing when she realized God could fulfill His purpose for her exactly the way she was.

"Well, it helped me a lot. And I started to think about what it is about you that makes me appreciate you so much."

Christy felt a little funny having Sierra shower her with such praise.

"You know what you do?" Sierra asked. "You love people. Gently, calmly, with specific, kind attention, you make people feel welcome. You put people at ease that way, Christy. It's a gift. I think God has given you the gift of hospitality as well as organization."

Christy took in Sierra's words. "I don't know about the hospitality part. I don't exactly live in a place where I can do a lot of entertaining. I never have. And being married to Todd, I have a feeling a house with lots of guest rooms isn't going to be in my future."

"Who needs a house? I'm talking about your heart. You have plenty of guest rooms there. And that's what you do. You open your heart to people. You keep lovely little rooms in there, just waiting for your friends to come visit. People feel as if they can come right in, just as they are. You don't entertain, you love. That's what lasts. That's why people like me feel as if I will always be your friend. You hold a special place for me in your heart."

Tears rolled down Christy's cheeks faster than she could blink them away. "Thank you, Sierra. Thank you."

"Don't thank me, thank God. He's the One who gifted you the way He did." Sierra flashed a bright, free-as-a-kite smile at Christy and hopped up from the chair. "It looks like those guys have already ordered. I better go. See you later."

Christy felt that a great life mystery had just been solved. She knew who she was, she knew how God had gifted her, and she felt peace coming over her like a cozy down comforter.

Wherever Todd and I end up living, however I end up using this college degree, I now know what my life is about. I can love people. I am a woman of hospitality. A woman who loves.

CHRISTY AND TODD
THE COLLEGE YEARS

As the final weeks of Christy's senior year slid past, her
16 life seemed to fall into place. She felt her
future was more defined. Sierra's words
about Christy's spiritual gift being hospitality had opened up a world of understanding and possibilities to her. She liked being hos-
pitable, and she thought being organized and detail
oriented were nice companions to hospitality. It all
made sense. Now she knew what her life was about,
and she was eager to move forward, being true to the
person God had created her to be.

The wedding plans were also coming together
nicely. Their bank account was growing, thanks to
Todd's painting job, and Christy was finding time to
complete her class work since she rarely saw Todd.

On the Friday afternoon before Easter vacation,
Christy worked extra hours in the bookstore while the
other student employees left early for their vacations.
Matthew Kingsley came in wearing a baseball cap over
his light brown hair. He appeared to have grown an

inch since she had seen him last.

"Hi," Christy said.

"Hi yourself." His warm brown eyes smiled down at her. "Where have you been hiding? I haven't seen you in weeks. I stopped by a couple of times, but you haven't been here."

"My hours changed this semester," Christy said. "I have more classes, too. I've been swamped."

"Tell me about it. They have us on a crazy schedule this baseball season."

"How are you doing?"

"Great. My mom told me about your grandfather passing away," Matt said. "I was real sorry to hear that. He was a good man."

Matt and Christy had grown up together in Brightwater. He had been her first crush at Washington Elementary School, and now they were at the same school again. Last semester Christy had seen Matt all the time. This semester they rarely ran into each other.

"Thanks, Matt," Christy said. "I agree. He was a wonderful man. I saw your sisters at the funeral. They've really grown."

"Yeah, they're both doing well. My family is coming to California this summer, so they're pretty excited."

"Are you staying here this summer?"

Matt nodded. "I got a job with the Youth Outreach Center. That's why I haven't been helping Todd with the youth group at his church. I have my own bunch of kids to work with now. They're a lot more street smart than the kids Todd works with. I like it. We have two baseball teams put together so far."

"That sounds like something you would be good at," Christy said. "How did you find that job?"

"Jenna works there. She recommended me."

"Jenna?"

"Don't you remember Jenna? I told you guys in the cafeteria one day in December that I wanted to ask her out, and you talked me into that group date event at The Dove's Nest."

"Oh yes, Jenna."

"It's okay if you don't remember much about that night. You and Todd were pretty busy getting yourselves engaged."

Christy smiled. "That was a special night. I was glad you were there."

Matt hesitated and shyly looked over his shoulder before saying, "We're still doing stuff together."

"You are? You and Jenna?"

Matt nodded.

"Good for you! She seemed like a really sweet person."

"She is," Matt said. "I've been wanting to tell you that because, well . . . I guess I just wanted you to know and to be happy for me. You're like the closest thing to family I have here."

"I'm glad you told me. I hope you bring her to our wedding. The invitations haven't been mailed yet, but it's on May twenty-second."

"I'll be there," Matt said. "And I'll bring Jenna with me."

"Good." Christy hoped her warm smile told Matt how happy she was for him.

"As a matter of fact, Jenna and I are going bowling tonight, in case you and Todd want to go with us."

"Bowling, huh?" Christy thought it was great Matt had found a girl who liked sports. "Thanks, but I'm not sure we can squeeze it in. As soon as I get off work, I have to drive down to my parents' house. The brides-maids' dresses arrived, and I have to get Tracy's to her in case it needs altering."

"Oh." Matt nodded but looked as if he had no idea what she was talking about. "We can try to do something together another time."

"Sure." Christy knew it wouldn't happen. At least not in the next two months.

Maybe after we're married, Todd and I will find time to get our social life back.

On Saturday afternoon, Christy drove to Carlsbad with Tracy's bridesmaid's dress in the Volvo's backseat. She and Tracy planned to meet for lunch at the Blue Ginger Café, but Christy was a little early. That was fine with her because she was able to grab an open table outside where the fresh spring sunshine poured over her, warming her and making her eager for summer to come. She closed her menu and closed her eyes, basking in the warmth.

A few moments later, Tracy walked up, and Christy smiled to see her friend's little belly pooching out in a compact, round ball.

"I know," Tracy said, patting her tummy. "I'm definitely showing."

"You look so cute! You're adorable." Christy hugged her and patted the baby bubble gently. "You look really good, Tracy."

"Thanks, Christy. I can't say that I believe you, but thanks." Tracy pulled out a chair and sat across from Christy. "Have you ordered yet?"

"No, I was just enjoying a little sunshine break."

"It's nice today, isn't it? I hope you didn't wait long. We had an appointment with the doctor before coming here, and it lasted longer than we expected. He had some surprising news for us."

Christy took off her sunglasses to see Tracy's face more clearly. "Twins?"

"No." Tracy laughed nervously. "Thank goodness! We found out it's a boy. We want to name him Daniel."

"That's wonderful! Or were you hoping for a girl?"

"No, I'm thrilled. Doug is thrilled."

"And you like the name Daniel?"

"I love it. He can go by Danny when he's little and then use Daniel when he earns his Ph.D."

Christy grinned. "You have high aspirations for this child."

"Doesn't every parent?"

The waitress stepped up to their table, and they both ordered garden salads and sparkling mineral water.

"Are we becoming old ladies or what?" Christy asked. "Look at us, ordering salads and mineral water.

That's what my aunt would order."

"I talked to your aunt this week," Tracy said.

"You did?"

"Yes. I have some more news for you. I've been planning a couple's shower for you and Todd. Doug thought we should make it a surprise, but I told him I was going to tell you today because I thought it would be easier if you knew."

"Thanks, Tracy."

"It's this Thursday, and your aunt volunteered her house because, when Doug and I started to make a list of people to invite, we realized we couldn't fit twenty or more people in our little living room."

"And my aunt agreed to this?"

"She was thrilled and honored. I told her we would do all the food, but she insisted I let her take care of everything because of my 'condition.'" Tracy settled back in her chair and rested her arm on her stomach. "I would have argued with her, but the truth is, I am pretty tired all the time."

"Todd said you were planning to quit your job after the baby . . . or should I say, after Danny gets here."

Tracy nodded and sipped the mineral water the waitress placed in front of her. "We might have to move."

"Why? You have a darling house."

"I know. But our lease is up in November, and it's so small. We only have the one bedroom. That's fine while Daniel is tiny, but he's going to need his own room eventually."

"I hadn't thought about that," Christy said. "Would you move into a two-bedroom apartment or what?"

"I don't know. It's something we've just started to talk about. Doug has this dream about buying a house, getting a dog, and having a backyard big enough for a swing set. We would have to move inland to afford that."

"I imagine you would miss the beach a lot."

"Yes," Tracy said. "But you would be surprised. We hardly ever go to the beach anymore. When we first moved there, we went all the time. I guess we need to be more responsible and frugal and live in an area that's less expensive."

Christy swished the ice and mineral water in her glass. "Who knows? We might end up in the same neighborhood."

"Are you and Todd going to live near Rancho?" Tracy asked.

"We're working on finding an apartment in the same complex where Rick lives, if you can believe that. It's only about five minutes from the church."

"I'll have to convince Doug to check out that area. He was saying last night that we should move to Oregon because he knows a guy who lives in a small town there, and we could afford to buy a house."

After the waitress arrived with their salads, Christy offered to give thanks before they ate. They chatted about everything, from the upcoming shower and Christy's wedding plans to how it felt the first time Tracy felt little Danny kicking inside her. As Christy inconspicuously picked the walnut pieces out of her salad, she thought of how this was the most relaxing, enjoyable two hours in the sunshine she had spent in months. She hoped Doug and Tracy didn't move to Oregon. She needed Tracy to be nearby after Christy was married so they could make time for more relaxing afternoons like this.

When they walked to the parking lot so Christy could give Tracy her dress, Tracy asked about Rick and Katie.

"They're doing great," Christy said. "Katie is taking it nice and slow, and Rick is treating her the way she deserves to be treated."

"Do you think they'll end up together?" Tracy asked. "I mean, do you think they'll get married?"

Christy thought a moment. "I wouldn't be surprised. Katie is determined to finish college, and I haven't talked to her about it, but I would guess she and Rick would opt for a fairly short engagement."

"Does that seem amazing to you?" Tracy asked.

"I guess, if I think about it long enough. It seems right, though. It seems evident the Lord is fulfilling His purpose for each of us."

"Yes, He is," Tracy agreed with a contented sigh.

On Thursday night Todd left work early for their couple's shower. When he arrived at the dorm to pick up Christy, he had on a freshly ironed, short-sleeved Hawaiian-print shirt and khaki shorts. He hugged Christy, and she could tell he had shaved and used a deep moss- and plum-scented cologne.

"You look great!" Christy said. "And you smell great, too."

Todd held her hand and led her to the car. "It's Rick's aftershave. What do you think?"

"It's nice."

"Rick ironed the shirt for me. He's pretty domestic."

Christy thought that was a good thing since she couldn't remember ever seeing Katie iron.

"You look really nice." Todd wrapped his arm around Christy's waist and drew her close. "I like that skirt on you. I don't know if I told you that the last time you wore it. It looks good on you."

"Thanks. Are you hungry? Do you want to stop and get something to eat before we drive to Newport Beach?"

"No, I'm fine. How about you?"

"No, I'm not hungry."

They got in the Volvo, which was parked all by itself in a nearly empty parking lot. "This hasn't been much of an Easter vacation for you, has it?" Todd asked. "Are you wishing you hadn't stayed on campus?"

"It was the best thing for me, really," Christy said. "I've worked twenty-two hours so far this week doing inventory in the bookstore. The income is going to help us a lot. And I'm nearly finished with my second paper. After that I only have two more to write. Finals are in three and a half weeks, and then I'm done!"

"I'm proud of you, Kilikina. Have I ever told you that? You were right about needing time to plan our wedding. I'm amazed at how much you've accomplished on top of finishing your final semester of school. If I had been at all understanding, I would have agreed to get married in August like you wanted so you wouldn't have had all this pressure on top of finishing school."

"It hasn't been too much," Christy said. "It's been a lot, but as long as I haven't tried to fit a social life in on top of everything, it's been okay."

"I know," Todd agreed as he drove onto the freeway. "We haven't been able to see each other very much, have we?"

"That will change soon enough," Christy said. "This is only a season for us. A short season. I think we're doing pretty well, don't you?"

"I do. So tell me," Todd said. "What do people do at a shower?"

"Sometimes they play games. Then we eat and open presents."

The whole concept seemed foreign to Todd. "What kind of games?"

"You know, little word-circling games on paper or dressing up the bride with toilet paper to form a wedding dress and veil."

"And this is going to be fun, right?"

Christy laughed. "You'll have a good time, Todd. At least you better. You're the guest of honor."

Todd nodded. He ran his fingers through his short hair. "By any chance, have these guys said anything about doing anything at the shower tonight?"

Christy finally understood why Todd was acting so nervous. He was expecting to be kidnapped at the shower the way he and the other guys had kidnapped Doug at his bachelor's party. They had taken Doug to the Balboa ferry, made him wear a chicken costume, and then chained him to the boat.

Suppressing a grin, Christy said, "Why do you ask?"

"Just wondering."

Christy hadn't heard any talk about the guys planning to kidnap Todd. But then, she guessed they wouldn't tell her their plans.

"I'm sure my aunt and uncle will keep this party under control."

"But it's being hosted by Doug and Tracy, right?"

"Yes, it is."

Todd looked worried. Christy tried not to giggle.

When Todd and Christy arrived at Bob and Marti's,
Christy found Tracy in the living room
trying to pick up a name tag from the
floor. But she seemed to find the task a
challenge.

"I can get that." Christy bent effortlessly and placed
the tag in the basket slung over Tracy's arm.

"Thank you. I gave up tying my shoes," Tracy said.
"I had to buy these slip-on loafers yesterday because
my feet are so swollen. I'm not at my best as a pregnant woman."

"You look radiant," Todd said.

Christy turned to look at her kind fiancé.

He leaned over and kissed Tracy on the cheek. "I
mean that, Trace. I think you look good as a pregnant
woman. You have a glow on your face. I think you're
beautiful."

Tracy looked as if she might cry. "Thank you, Todd."

Oh, you sweet man! I hope you remember to say all those

wonderful things to me someday when my belly swells up twice the size of a basketball!

"I didn't hear you two come in," Marti said, bustling into the living room. "Tracy, dear, shouldn't you sit down?"

"I'm okay." Tracy shot Christy a look that said, "Just wait until it's your turn to be pregnant!"

"Todd, dear, Robert would like to see you in the garage."

"What about?" Todd's question came out with an edge to it.

Marti looked offended. "He needs help with a table. I'll go with you, Todd. Come."

Todd gave Christy a "farewell forever" glance and slowly headed to the garage.

Christy whispered to Tracy, "Todd thinks the guys are going to kidnap him tonight and do something wild, the way they kidnapped Doug and chained him to the ferry."

"Would my precious husband ever do such a thing?"

"Your precious husband isn't the one I'm worried about," Christy said. "One man alone isn't a threat. It's when all these men start brainstorming that I worry— especially with Rick back in the picture."

Todd and Doug marched into the living room, each carrying the end of a banquet-sized folding table. "Marti wants the gifts set up on this table," Doug said. "She said to put it in front of the window. Could you move that rocking chair, Christy?"

They all pitched in to set up the living room the way Aunt Marti wanted it. Doug didn't seem to be scheming anything on the side. Although, who could tell with Doug? His face always had an impish grin on it.

The guests began to arrive, and Marti greeted each one. She kept Tracy by her side with the basket of name tags and made sure each guest pinned on the proper tag. The black ones cut in the shape of a groom, complete with top hat, had the guys' names written in white ink. The white paper cutouts of a bride in a full skirt had the girls' names written in black ink. Christy thought the idea was cute but kind of funny, too, since everyone at the shower knew one another. No one was going to try to crash the party only to have Marti look in the basket and say, "No, sorry. I don't see a little groom with your name on it. Go away!"

The first game Marti directed was the one Christy had expected. The girls had five minutes to dress Christy as a bride with several rolls of toilet paper while the guys watched. Sierra single-handedly made the veil, which generated the most laughs. She snagged a roll of Scotch tape and somehow managed to make the strips of the veil stick straight out every which way.

Christy saw her reflection in the living room window and said, "Sierra, I look like the Statue of Liberty!"

The living room filled with waves of laughter. Several camera flashes went off as friends captured the moment on film. Christy stood patiently, letting it all roll over her. It was fun.

Todd, however, looked as nervous as a cat when he was called up to stand beside Christy. The guys were to dress him as the groom with rolls of toilet paper. Todd shot a glance at Christy as if he expected at any moment to have a gunnysack thrown over his head, to be hauled out the front door, hoisted into a cargo plane, and flown to Aruba.

All that happened was that Todd was wrapped up like a mummy with toilet paper strapping down his arms and covering his mouth, ears, and eyes. Doug joked that this was the truth about married life and for a final twist taped a wad of T.P. to Todd's chest that looked like a boutonniere.

Christy thought Todd looked hilarious all wrapped up, but she could tell by his nervous shuffling that he didn't like being the center of attention, and he certainly didn't like being blinded from any potential gunnysacks coming his way.

A few cameras flashed as Christy stood beside Todd with her wild-woman wedding veil and her bouquet of tissue balls. Her reluctant mummy broke out of his graveclothes and pulled the tissue off his eyes and mouth.

"Is that the last game?" he muttered to Christy as he peeled his cocoon and left the remains on the floor in a heap.

"I hope so." Christy gave his muscular arm three squeezes.

It wasn't enough to calm him. They were told to sit on the love seat by the gift table and to open the gifts. Todd looked behind the couch, apparently checking to make sure no one was hiding there.

As Christy opened each gift, she warmly thanked the giver, making a point to comment on something special about each item. It was easy to praise Tracy for the gift she gave, a charming, pudgy china teapot covered with red cabbage roses.

"It's like the one we used at that teahouse in England," Tracy said. "Remember, when you and I went to tea?"

"Of course I remember. Thanks, Trace. I love it."

An image came to Christy that she knew would be humorous only to her. She saw herself heating up water on their camp stove and serving tea to Tracy from this beautiful china pot while sitting on the surfboard sofa. If she wore her wedding dress at the same time, she could have her picture taken and send it to a bridal magazine with the caption, "Outback bride at tea time."

Todd's gifts included tools, a frying pan, and toenail clippers as a joke from Rick. They received bath towels, a salad bowl, and an ice-cream scoop that played an ice-cream-truck melody when you pushed a button on the handle.

"We need one of those at The Dove's Nest," Katie told Rick.

"I don't think so." He grinned at her in response.

Christy noticed how cute they looked snuggled up

next to each other. No one seemed to think their be-
havior unusual except for Marti. During the refresh-
ments, she pulled Christy aside. "Just what is happening with Rick and Katie?"

Christy wanted to say, "God is fulfilling His purpose
for them," but she hesitated. Marti didn't deserve a
flippant answer when she was asking a genuine question.

"They are getting to know each other better,"
Christy said.

"How much better?" Marti raised an eyebrow.

Sierra had been standing next to them and entered
into the conversation. "You know about the unwritten
rule at Rancho, don't you?"

"No," Marti said, falling for Sierra's little joke.

"For every upper-class woman the guarantee is 'a
ring by spring or your money back.' "

Marti didn't find that humorous. "They certainly
aren't planning to get engaged any time soon, are
they?"

"I don't know," Christy said. "You could ask Katie."

"No, I wouldn't ask such a thing. Really, Christina!
A person's love life is a personal matter."

"Besides," Sierra said, "I've discovered that when
two people are meant to be together, you can't do anything to break them up. And if they aren't meant to be
together, you can't do anything to keep them together."

Both Christy and Marti looked at Sierra, who was
tucking a small strawberry into her mouth. Sierra

turned to talk to someone else. Her wild mane of un-
ruly blond curls followed her.

"Honestly," Marti said, "some of your friends are
such . . ."

"Individuals?" Christy offered.

"Yes, individuals and uncontrollable."

Christy smiled. "I like my friends that way. They're
good for me."

Even though Marti wasn't happy at the moment,
she had worn a pleased expression when Christy and
Todd had opened the last gift, which was from Bob and
Marti. It was two place settings of china in the pattern
Christy had selected weeks ago while shopping with
Marti and her mom. Todd didn't seem too apprecia-
tive, but Christy knew what the gift cost and made
sure she expressed her delight to her aunt.

She thanked Aunt Marti again when Todd and
Christy were about to leave. "It was a wonderful
shower." Christy kissed Marti's cheek. "The food was
delicious, and I love the china. Thank you so much for
everything."

"You sure you kids don't want to stay the night?"
Bob asked. "It's pretty late for you to be driving."

"I have to start work at seven in the morning,"
Todd said. "I think we'll be okay. Thanks again for
everything. Thanks, too, for letting us keep all the gifts
here until we get our apartment."

"No problem. Drive safely," Bob replied.

"We will."

"Bye." Christy blew them a kiss and headed down

the sidewalk with Todd. She glanced above the house's roof and noticed a full moon gracing the deep night sky.

"We love you both," Marti called out.

Then Christy saw her aunt slip her arm around Uncle Bob's waist and rest her head on his shoulder as she waved to them. The grin that lit up Uncle Bob's face was as bright as the full moon winking at Christy from the heavens above.

She winked back. It was a perfect night for relentless lovers to do their wooing.

Just as Christy and Todd reached their car, a wild war cry sounded. The party guests, who supposedly had left, came rushing at Todd and Christy from behind cars and bushes.

Todd grabbed Christy and tried to protect her from whatever kind of attack was coming their way. All around them Silly String rained down. Dozens of canisters went off at the same moment as their friends circled them, and each squirted two cans over Todd and Christy. The laughing and squealing filled the night air. Christy laughed at Todd, who responded like a zealous Scottish warrior, protecting Christy with one arm and fending off the volley of Silly String with the other. Brightly colored string covered the couple; their friends were gleefully victorious.

Todd decided on the way home that if that was the worst prank to be played on him, he had gotten off easy. During the month that followed, it appeared that was the case.

The day Christy donned her cap and gown and received her college diploma, she found a glob of fluorescent green and orange Silly String in her good pair of shoes. It was also the day she started to sneeze and to experience itching eyes and a dripping nose. Her graduation ceremony and the following celebration dinner with her extended family and friends turned out to be a repeat of Todd's graduation event, with most of the same people in attendance. Only at hers, Christy sneezed like crazy.

Marti suggested Christy might have allergies since she had never lived in that area before. Different pollens existed there than the ones Christy had been acclimated to in Escondido, Marti pointed out.

Her mother commented that Christy had dark circles under her eyes and asked if she wanted to go home that night.

"I think I'll stick with the original plan," Christy said. "I'll stay in the dorm tonight and try to sleep in. Tomorrow I'll move all my things to Todd's apartment."

"Our apartment," Todd corrected her. They had secured a one-bedroom apartment in the same complex Rick lived in. Todd had moved his belongings over a few days ago, but Christy's handful of worldly possessions was still in her dorm room.

The past month had been a blur of writing papers, taking finals, working on last-minute wedding plans, interviewing for jobs, and never seeing Todd. If she had dark circles under her eyes, she knew she didn't need to blame them on an allergy. But it was over. She had made it. Now she was a college graduate. It felt good. A little too smoothly orchestrated perhaps to be as memorable as she had thought it would be, but then, she had another major event looming ahead in nine short days.

"Okay, how about this plan," Christy suggested to her mom as they left the restaurant. "I'll take some allergy medicine, get a good night's sleep in my dorm room, move my things into our apartment tomorrow morning, and then come home. You can baby me all you want."

Her plan worked fairly well. The allergy medication helped her to sleep a full ten hours, which was a rare occurrence. She didn't wake up the next morning until after eight. Within two minutes she discovered the one night's dosage of allergy pills hadn't relieved her of the sneezing. At least she felt rested.

Katie returned from her morning shower and said, "Hey, sleeping beauty, what's on your schedule?"

Christy tried to say, "Katie, I'm getting married in eight days," but her nose was so stuffed up the thought came out, "Katie, I'b gettin' barried in eight days."

"Yes, you are," Katie said with a laugh. "And aren't you going to be a lovely bride."

"I'll be better by den." Christy noticed her cap and gown hanging on the hook above her closet. It didn't seem as if she actually had graduated. The whole day had gone by so fast. She hoped her wedding day would go more slowly and remain more memorable.

Classes were still going for those who hadn't graduated, and Katie pointed out she had to take a final. "Will you be here when I get back?"

"I don't know. Todd is going to borrow Matt's truck so we can take our lovely surfin' sofa to the apartment. I'm not sure when he's coming."

"He called before I took my shower," Katie said. "He said he wasn't coming because a painting job opened up this morning. He said he talked to Matt, and Matt can take your stuff over at ten."

"That's some improvement," Christy said with a sigh before blowing her nose. "At least he calls now."

"Do you want me to go with you guys and help? I don't have to be at work until this afternoon."

"That would be wonderful."

"I'll meet you back here at ten," Katie said.

"Thanks, Katie. I'll take a hot shower and try some more allergy medication."

At 9:45 Sierra showed up. "Hi. How are you feeling?" Sierra held out a bottle of orange juice to Christy. "I saw Katie, and she said you weren't sounding very good."

"Thanks for the juice. I think it's allergies," Christy said. "Please don't tell my aunt. She enjoys it way too much when she's right. I'm feeling lots better now."

"Do you need some help moving your things?" Sierra asked.

"That would be great. Matt should be here in a little

while. I have everything packed. When he comes, you can help us load his truck."

Christy opened the orange juice and took a drink. "Are you getting excited about going to Brazil?"

"I think so," Sierra said. "I still have finals to finish up. Not that you would know anything about that."

"Oh, a little."

"Is everything ready for your wedding?" Sierra asked.

"You know, amazingly enough, I think so. Everything on the list has been taken care of, thanks to my mom and my aunt. Todd and I finished our premarital counseling sessions, and they really were helpful. We got into the apartment we wanted, and everything should run like clockwork a week from tomorrow. We just have a few details about our future to work out, but we'll do that after the honeymoon."

Just then the phone rang. It was Donna, Christy's boss from the campus bookstore.

"Oh good. I'm glad I caught you," she said. "I wanted you to know that I have your final check here, in case you would like to stop by to pick it up today."

"That would be great. Thanks, Donna."

"Sure. And I have a question for you. This is a little out of the ordinary, I know, and you don't have to answer me right away. I'm resigning from the campus bookstore in two weeks."

"Oh?"

"I was offered a position as the manager of another bookstore, and I've decided to take it. I need to hire an

assistant manager at my new job, and you were recommended by the owner."

"I was?" Christy had placed her resume at several
businesses around town, but she didn't think she had
met any of the owners.

"My new position is at The Ark. Mrs. Doyle said you
were good friends with her son. He runs the café next
door."

Christy felt like laughing. "Yes, we are good friends.
I put in a resume there a month ago, but the manager
said they were in transition."

"I guess I'm part of the transition," Donna said.
"Think about it. Pray about it. I'd love to have you as
my assistant manager."

"Okay," Christy said. "It would be perfect for me.
But I couldn't start until after the first of June."

"That's fine because I start on June first," Donna
said. "Let me know what you think. I'll see you at your
wedding, if not before."

"Thanks, Donna."

"Sure."

Christy turned to Sierra. "It looks like I have a job
after we get back from our honeymoon. I was going to
tell you, before the phone rang, that one of the unsettled details was that I didn't have a job. I think God
took care of that in record time."

"Hey, kids, how's it going?" Katie entered the room
and tossed an apple at Christy. "This is for you,
roomie. I worried about your taking allergy medicine
on an empty stomach."

"Thanks."

"You guys ready to rock and roll?" Katie asked.

"Matt isn't here yet," Christy said. "But guess what? It looks like I have a job."

She told Katie the details while Katie stared at the boxes neatly stacked on Christy's side of the room.

"Don't leave me," Katie said.

Sierra laughed. "Didn't you hear Christy? She just said she's going to work in the bookstore next to you. You guys will see each other every day."

"We'll probably see each other more than we did this past semester," Christy said.

"I know," Katie said wistfully. "But at least stay in the dorm until I'm done next week, and we can move out together. This is too sad. Look at your side of the room. It's empty."

"It went fast, didn't it?" Christy said.

Katie sat on the edge of her unmade bed, the bed that had gone unmade the entire school year except for the rare occasion when Christy convinced Katie to wash the sheets.

"Do you two remember the week before school started?" Sierra asked. "The three of us were sitting in here, telling each other our woes."

"I remember," Katie said. "It's been a full year."

"It certainly has," Christy agreed.

"You know what?" Sierra said. "I think we should pray."

"Good idea," Christy said.

The three friends stood in a close circle and looped

their arms over each other's shoulders. They prayed sweet, rich words of thankfulness and bold requests for God's future blessings.

When they finished, Christy said, "I love you both. You know that, don't you?"

A tentative knock sounded on their door. Katie let in Matt and in a melancholy voice said, "I guess this is it. Go ahead, Matt. Take her stuff. I always knew she loved Todd more than she loved me."

CHRISTY AND TODD
THE COLLEGE YEARS

18 Matt went to work clearing Christy's dorm room like the strong, steady farm boy he was. Christy, Katie, and Sierra carried Christy's boxes out to the curb while he wrestled the surfin' sofa into the back of his truck. Katie led the way to the apartment in Baby Hummer, and for the first time, Christy unlocked the front door with her very own key.

She didn't know whether to laugh or cry when she peered inside. Todd should have been there to carry her over the threshold or something. Instead, she was standing with her friends, staring into an empty apartment. Christy realized she had created a fantasy of what she thought her first home with Todd would be like. In her dreams, it was a cottage with a fireplace and flowers all in a row along the walkway.

"Where do you want this stuff?" Katie asked.

"Anywhere," Christy said. "There's plenty of room."

It took them only two trips to empty the truck. Matt adjusted the surfin' sofa in the middle of the living room and said he needed to get back to school to finish a paper.

"Thanks so much," Christy said.

"I'll see you next Saturday," he said.

"I'm going to go back with him." Sierra gave Christy a hug. "I'll email you from Brazil."

"I'll email back," Christy promised.

Matt and Sierra left, and Katie stood with her hand on her hip looking around the apartment. "This is a bit bleak, isn't it?"

"It'll cheer up once I put some pictures on the wall," Christy said.

"Or maybe add a stick or two of furniture."

A tear trickled down Christy's cheek.

"Oh, I didn't mean to hurt your feelings," Katie said. "You guys will fix it up. You'll get a bunch of wedding presents, and you'll find a real couch and a kitchen table. It'll be wonderful. You're just starting out."

Christy sniffed. "I need flowers, Katie."

"Flowers?"

"Yes, flowers in a pot by the front door. And maybe a welcome mat. That's what I need."

"Say no more. I was wondering what I could buy you for a housewarming present, and now I know. Come on, let's buy a flower and a welcome mat."

An hour later, Katie and Christy returned to the apartment all smiles with a bright, cheery potted daisy and a welcome mat. They also had a box of tissues, six homemade chocolate-chip cookies from the bakery, a bottle of liquid soap, and a bottle of lotion to put by the kitchen sink.

"Now it's home," Christy said, arranging her new treasures.

"You certainly are easy to please," Katie said.

"Todd is the minimalist. I don't require much, but the few necessities I do need are paramount."

"I wish I could stay and help you put pictures on the wall, but I have to run. Are you going to be okay?"

"Yes, I'll be fine. When Todd gets home, he's going to drive me down to my parents'."

"Did you hear what you just said?" Katie asked. "You said when Todd gets home. It worked. You do see this as your new home."

Christy reminded herself of Katie's comment as she unpacked her boxes and checked out the kitchen cupboards. She found three paper cups, one coffee mug, and a stack of paper plates. She rinsed out the coffee mug, filled it with water, heated it in the microwave, and made herself a comforting cup of tea.

Looking for the tissue to blow her nose, she found Katie had put the box in the bathroom. Christy stood there blowing her nose and noticed a big glob of toothpaste in the sink. The towel was on the floor instead of on the towel rack. Todd had been living here.

Continuing her tour into the bedroom, she was relieved to see their new bed had arrived. Todd had slept on the floor in a sleeping bag when he first had moved in. His dad offered to buy a bed as his wedding present to them, and they both gratefully accepted.

The comfy-looking bed was set up in the small bedroom, but it didn't have a headboard or any sheets on it. One rather worn wool army blanket lay at the foot of the bed. The blanket looked like a World War II relic, which was depressing. But noticing it was folded, Christy felt hopeful Todd might be a little tidier than the evidence in the bathroom suggested.

Todd had a dresser; Christy had a bookcase and a chair.

This is more pathetic than I realized. We are really poor.

Christy went to work unpacking her boxes and deciding on which empty wall she should hang her few pictures and posters. She worked quickly and had all her boxes unpacked in short order. She filled up the bookshelf, put her small rug in front of the kitchen sink, and hung the poster of the waterfall with the memorable bridge on the wall in the kitchen. The splash of color did the apartment a world of good. She dusted off the top of Todd's dresser and placed her framed pictures of the two of them next to the only item Todd had on the dresser, the picture she had given him for his birthday.

All that was left to unpack was the box with her yellow patchwork blanket, a useless set of twin sheets, two bath towels, her pillow, and a treasure she knew she wanted to keep with her always. It was her old pal Pooh, the stuffed Winnie the Pooh Todd had bought her at Disneyland. Pooh had held her secrets and wiped her tears for too many years to be left in a box in her parents' closet. She hoped Todd would understand.

Christy carried her yellow quilt into the bedroom. The bed looked so inviting. She stretched out, tucked Pooh under her arm, and pulled her blanket up over both of them. Settling in on the right side of the bed, Christy wondered if Todd preferred the right side. Or would they sleep together in the middle every night, wrapped in each other's arms?

Through her fuzzy head floated puffy, fluffy, happy dreams like summer clouds coasting through a deep blue sky. And that was the last thing she remembered.

Many hours later, Christy woke. She didn't recall where she was at first. Then it all came tumbling over her. She looked toward the bedroom doorway and gave a startled gasp when she saw Todd standing there, watching her as she slept.

He was leaning against the doorjamb, arms folded across his chest, a gentle smile on his face.

"Hey, how's it going?" That phrase, that voice, had echoed for half a decade through Christy's waking hours and in her dreams. For a moment she wasn't sure if she was awake or if this was part of her dream.

"How long have you been standing there?"

"Awhile. I took a shower. The noise didn't wake you?"

"No."

"You have no idea how beautiful you are when you're sleeping, Kilikina."

Christy wanted to hold out her arms to her beloved, inviting Todd to come to her and hold her. But she didn't move.

Todd didn't move, either. It was as if they were once again at an intersection in their lives. In the early years, the red lights had been there to give Todd and Christy a quick chance for a kiss and a memory. Today an invisible red light did the opposite. It kept them from kissing. Christy knew Todd felt what she was feeling. God was controlling the traffic lights at the intersections. He would change the light to green in eight short days. Until then, it would be foolish to run a red light.

"How are you feeling?"

"I'm okay." Christy tossed back the comforter, and Pooh tumbled to the floor. Christy didn't know if Todd noticed. "We have to be sure to thank your dad a thousand times. This is the most comfortable bed I've slept on in two years."

"The delivery guys came this morning," Todd said. "I see you brought your own blankie."

Christy folded her patchwork comforter. "My grandma made this. I've had it since elementary school."

"I never knew that," Todd said.

"I never knew you left your towel on the floor." Christy walked toward him.

"Uh-oh. Is that one of those issues they talked about in our premarital counseling? Should I hang up towels so that you feel more loved?"

"It wouldn't hurt," Christy said. "But I should confess that my last roommate never made her bed or hung up her towel, so perhaps Katie prepared me for you."

"How do those vows go, now? For better or worse? Richer or poorer?"

Christy stepped out of the bedroom. As soon as she stepped over the invisible line and stood on Todd's side, he wrapped his arms around her and hugged her close.

"I think we have the poorer part figured out," Christy said.

"Hey, I like all the Christy touches you added to our home. The flowers by the front door and the welcome mat are especially nice," Todd murmured. "Do you want to head out for your parents' house?"

"Yes, I think we better."

They both stayed at her parents' that night. Once again the allergy medication made Christy konk out. She woke in a Saturday-morning sort of daze and padded out to the kitchen in her pj's, robe, and slippers.

The house was silent. Pouring herself a bowl of cereal, she sat down at the kitchen table. A moment later Todd and David walked into the kitchen. Christy instinctively clutched the top of her robe. She knew she looked awful. Her hair was going in every direction, and she needed a shower.

"Morning, beautiful," Todd said.

"I look terrible!" Christy squeaked. She could tell by the expression on David's face he agreed with her evaluation.

If you can call me beautiful when I look like this, my soon-to-be husband, then you'll be in for a nice surprise next Saturday.

"We're going to the skate park for an hour or so," Todd said. "When I get back, you can give me the final to-do list."

"Okay." Christy tried to tuck her stringy hair behind her ears.

"See ya," David said as they marched past her.

The door to the garage closed. A moment later it opened, and Todd's face appeared around the corner, wearing a boyish grin. "Hey, you in the bathrobe and fuzzy slippers, if you're not doing anything next Saturday, what do you think? You want to get married?"

Christy grinned and held out her arms to provide Todd a full view of her frumpy robe, flannel pj's, and disheveled hair. "For better or worse," she said.

"From where I'm standing, I'm thinking it can only get better by next Saturday. At least I'm hopin'."

Christy took off one of her fuzzy slippers and heaved it at him. He shut the door just in time for the slipper to miss its target.

Christy returned to her bowl of cereal, laughing to herself. She thought back to their first date to Disneyland when she had thrown her sandal at him.

She hadn't realized her mother had stepped into the living room and was watching the scene. Mom looked surprised, as if she hadn't seen this side of her daughter before.

"Don't worry, Mom. He was laughing."

Mom shook her head. "I shouldn't wonder, dear. You really should have a look in the mirror."

One very short week later, Christy heard her mother once again say, "You really should have a look in the mirror."

Only this time, no one was laughing at how Christy looked.

She was wearing her wedding dress and was standing in the middle of the living room of a hotel suite that Marti had rented close to Rancho Corona. At Marti's insistence, Bob and she had stayed overnight close to the college and then turned over the suite as a dressing room for Christy on the morning of May 22. Marti also had insisted Christy allow Marti's favorite hair and makeup artist to come at eleven so that, after Christy showered, she could have two hours set aside for what Marti called "beautification."

It was now one-thirty. The wedding was at three o'clock. Christy was ready. In every way, she was ready.

"Your gown turned out perfect." Katie adjusted the train in the back. "I'll make sure it's smoothed out like this when you stand under the arch."

Christy inched her way to the bedroom in the suite so she could have a look in the full-length mirror on the closet. Katie followed her, adjusting the train as Christy walked.

"Wait! Don't look until we put on your veil!" Marti bustled over to the refrigerator, where they had stored the flower wreath that arrived from Maui that morning.

"Close your eyes." Tracy came up alongside Christy and took her by the hand. "It will be better if you wait and have a look once your veil is on. Then you'll see for the first time what Todd is going to see when you come down the aisle toward him."

Christy closed her eyes and felt at peace. All the extra planning had paid off. Everything was coming together perfectly. Marti's extravagant pampering had been a blessing, and Christy had told her so several times.

At the rehearsal dinner the night before, Todd had stood beside his father and praised him in a kind and generous way. Todd's mother couldn't "work out the details" to come to the wedding. Everyone knew it was a last-minute letdown and silently had sympathized with Todd, but he seemed to handle the disappointment well.

After honoring his dad, Todd had turned to Bob and Marti and thanked them for being his honorary parents. He called Marti the "mom I never had," listing how she had been there at many key moments in his life as a teenager and a young adult. He told her he loved her and always would. He kissed her, and Marti cried.

Christy let Tracy lead her into the bedroom and position her in front of the mirror. She smelled her wreath of flowers before she felt Marti place it on her head. The sweet fragrance of the island tuberose filled her with exotic memories. She knew Todd would recognize the fragrance, as well. It would circle both of them as they repeated their vows.

"Bend down, Christy, dear. You're too tall for me," Marti said. "I don't want to ruin your hair. It's perfect. Absolutely perfect. That's it. A little lower."

Christy's grandmother spoke up. "Why don't you let Margaret help you with that?"

"I've got it," Marti stated firmly.

"Don't start an argument here," Katie teased.

Behind her closed eyes, Christy thought back on the argument she and Todd had two days ago. It was one of the worst they had ever had. More than five months ago, when they had decided they were going to say "I promise" instead of "I do," Christy and Todd had agreed they would write their own vows. Christy had worked on hers off and on for months and had finalized them before their last meeting with Pastor Ross, who was performing their ceremony.

Todd, however, as of two days ago, hadn't begun to work on his. When Christy found out, she fell apart. She said some awful things, Todd said some awful things, and for one frantic moment, Christy feared the whole wedding would be called off.

But they found their heads. Cleared their hearts. Talked calmly. Then they called Pastor Ross, and he made some helpful suggestions. In the end, they decided to repeat the traditional vows so that neither of them would go blank at the last minute while under the pressure of the ceremony. Christy decided she would place her personally created vows on a beautiful piece of stationery and make it her final entry into the shoebox of letters for her future husband.

That collection of letters, complete with her written-out vows, was wrapped with a white satin ribbon and tucked into the bottom of her honeymoon luggage, directly under her white lingerie. A smile played across her lips as Christy thought about all that this very special day and night would hold for her and her beloved.

"A little more to the right," Marti said. "Katie, fix that strand of hair over on her shoulder. We want to make sure all the beautiful embroidery shows perfectly. That's it. Okay, moisten your lips, dear. Good. Now everyone stand back. On the count of three, Christina, open your eyes."

Christy felt her heart do a little cha-cha as her eyelids fluttered, trying to remain closed.

In unison, the most precious women in her life began the countdown. "One, two . . ."

CHRISTY AND TODD · THE COLLEGE YEARS

"THREE!" the women-in-waiting cried with one voice and one heart.

19 Christy opened her eyes to view her reflection in the full-length mirror. The wreath of fragrant white island flowers graced her head like a crown of purity and peace. The delicate, sheer veil cascaded from the wreath and circled her shoulders like an elegant cape belonging to a fairy-tale princess who had made it from translucent firefly wings spun into the finest threads.

The wedding gown was indeed a gown and not just a dress. Christy's small waist and trim figure were accentuated by the wide band that united her mother's wedding dress with hers. The new version of both their dreams blended into one was exactly what Christy had hoped for. She knew it always would be one of her favorite parts of the wedding. The embroidery shimmered in the overhead lighting and drew attention to Christy's face.

She paused, catching her breath in amazement at

her own reflection. The makeup artist had done exactly what she had asked with her hair and face. She looked natural yet with a warm glow on her cheeks and a sparkle in her blue-green eyes. Her long, nutmeg brown hair was tucked behind her ears with shimmering clips, and two long, full curls danced down her bodice, just under her veil.

"Okay, I'm going to cry now," Christy said, breaking the silence.

They all laughed except for Marti. "Don't you dare! Your eye makeup is perfect!"

"Here," Christy's grandma sidled up next to her. "I was hoping for a good time to give you this. It's the handkerchief I carried at my wedding when I married your grandfather. His mother embroidered it for me. I want you to have it."

Now Christy was certain she would cry. She blinked quickly and, lifting her veil slightly, gave her grandmother a kiss on the cheek. "Thank you, Grandma. I love you."

"I know. And I love you, too."

"Katie," Marti called, "bring Christy's lipstick over here, quick. Mom, you have a smudge right on your cheek. Oh, was that a knock on the door? It must be the photographer. Everyone stay right where you are. I'll get it."

Marti hustled to answer the hotel suite's door. Christy took in a full view of her friends in their sky-blue bridesmaids' dresses. "You two look really nice. I love those dresses on you. The little baby's breath headbands turned out nice. Do you mind wearing them? Are they going to bug you?"

"Not at all," Tracy said.

"I like it." Katie handed Christy the lipstick. "Here you go. Or am I supposed to put it on you because I'm the maid of honor?"

"I can do it. You just hold on to it for me and make sure I reapply some before the photographer takes all the pictures after the wedding."

"Why?" Katie said with a grin. "Are you planning on getting your lipstick a little smeared there at the altar?"

"I sure did." Tracy exchanged a little grin with Katie and Christy.

"All right, ladies," Marti said. "Everyone step back so that our prompt photographer here can set up for the photos. Do you want Christy in here by the mirror or out in the living room?"

The photographer didn't move. He seemed to be sizing up the situation and more. His gaze was on Christy. "I'm sorry, what did you say?" he asked Marti.

"Where would you like her to stand?"

"This is fine." He set up his tripod and looked again at Christy. "I apologize for staring. But I have to say, I see brides all the time, but you are, well . . . you are one beautiful bride."

"Thank you." Christy blushed.

"I'll make some beautiful pictures for you."

"Oh dear!" Marti squeaked. "The bouquet! Where is the bouquet? Katie, find the bouquet."

With the bouquet in her hands and her lips freshly colored, Christy posed in her gorgeous wedding dress while the loving women in her life showered her with compliments and admiration. She shifted from her right foot to her left foot in the soft-soled ballet slippers she had decided to wear. They made her feel petite and dainty.

"Todd is going to be speechless," Tracy said. "I can't wait to see the look on his face when you come down the aisle toward him."

Me too!

"Now, Katie," Marti started in as they gathered their belongings and headed down to the lobby. "Do you have Todd's ring?"

"His ring?" Katie said playfully.

"Katie!"

Katie grinned and held up her thumb to show Marti that Todd's gold wedding band was safe with her.

"This isn't a time to joke. Come on, now; the limos are waiting."

Katie slipped behind Christy and lifted the train of Christy's gown. "The limos are waiting," Katie said in a ritzy voice. Then, breaking out in song, she serenaded Christy all the way to the elevator. "Going to the chapel . . ."

Christy loved Katie's lighthearted touches and told her so once she, Katie, Tracy, and her mom were tucked into the white stretch limo's backseat. Marti and Grandma said they were going to wait for Uncle Bob, who should be arriving at any minute. "All this posh fluff is for my aunt, not me," Christy said. "She's loving this. I'm enjoying it, too, but what I'm really enjoying is having the three of you with me."

Mom beamed. She looked radiant in her two-piece, cream-colored outfit. Marti's specialist had also done Mom's makeup, and it was the first time Christy remembered seeing her mom look extra fancy. She was a beautiful woman. Inside and out.

"When we get there," Katie said, "we have strict instructions to spirit you away to the chapel so nobody sees you. Especially your groom. So be prepared in case we have to make a dash for it. The closest the limo can get us is about a hundred yards from the path that leads to the meadow. We should be the first ones there, but just in case."

Christy nodded. "By any chance did you bring extra deodorant for me along with the lipstick and hairbrush?"

"It's all in the bridal basket in the trunk." Katie leaned forward as if they were in a football huddle. "Trace, why don't you grab the bridal basket and whatever else Marti put in the trunk. Christy, you take your bouquet and loop your train over your arm. Mom, you stay with me and be ready to haul biscuits if we have to make a dash for the chapel."

Christy laughed. "Katie, I don't think we're going to need to run like we're in a football game. There won't be anyone there yet."

However, when the limo parked on the upper campus at Rancho Corona University, Christy discovered she was wrong. Dozen of cars were aready parked in the lot, and her dad and David were standing by the pathway to the meadow in their tuxes.

"Aw, Mom, look! Don't they look adorable?"

"Adorable, schmorable!" Katie said, taking over as wedding director since Marti wasn't on the scene. "Grab your train and your bouquet and be ready to hotfoot it, missy. If two tuxedos are around here, there are bound to be more."

Christy willingly followed Katie's instructions, as did her mom and Tracy. When the limo driver opened the door, they stepped out and walked to the chapel at a brisk pace. Katie held on to Christy's elbow like a bodyguard, watching every which way for paparazzi. Christy looped her train over her arm, hitched up her skirt, and picked her way along the trail in her dainty ballet slippers.

"Christy," David called out. "Wait up!"

"Sorry," Katie called. "Can't stop. I'm under strict orders from your aunt. Got to deliver this woman to the chapel immediately!"

Christy felt like an elfin fairy, prancing down the meadow trail. She laughed at the bliss of it all and followed her illustrious maid of honor. Perky, red-haired Katie seemed to be the embodiment of a guardian angel, a heroic, celestial being.

But when they were three feet from the chapel's door, Katie stopped dead in her tracks. Christy nearly rear-ended her.

"Will you look at that?" Katie drew in a deep breath. "What a fine specimen of God's best creative efforts."

Christy followed Katie's gaze. Only a few yards away, Christy and Todd's enchanted meadow was alive with color and action. Bright streamer flags on top of each canopy waved at her in the afternoon breeze. Long tables, laden with fresh flowers and blue ribbons, were adorned with a variety of food fit for a grand celebration. In the forefront stood a round table under a canopy and on the table was the wedding cake. It looked exactly the way Christy had hoped it would look.

Rows of empty chairs waited for the wedding guests. All the chairs faced "their" arch, Todd and Christy's trellis archway that would serve as the symbolic entry to their lives' next season. Fresh flowers and deep green ferns adorned the archway. It looked as if it had grown in a hidden cove on a tropical island and had been picked up that morning and transplanted here, in the meadow, for their wedding. Christy knew Todd would be thrilled.

"It's wonderful!" Christy exclaimed to Katie after taking in the grand celebration being prepared. Along the edge, dozens of tall, swishy palm trees danced in the breeze like a row of hula dancers merrily sending their aloha over the event. "It's more wonderful than I had pictured it would be."

"What are you talking about?" Katie pulled her eyes off her target and looked at Christy. "I was saying that Rick is a fine specimen of God's best creative efforts.

He's standing over there talking to Todd's dad by the punch bowl. Oh no, what am I doing? You shouldn't be here! Look out, tuxedo at two o'clock."

Katie yanked open the chapel's door and practically pushed Christy inside the cool, quiet sanctuary.

"Katie, that wasn't Todd. That was Doug."

"Doesn't matter. If the best man is close, the groom won't be far away. Relax. Have a seat. Do you want some lipstick?"

"I am getting excited," Christy said, beaming.

"Nervous?"

"Not at all. Eager, yes. Bursting with anticipation, yes. This is it, Katie, girl. Todd and I are getting married today."

"So I heard," Katie said calmly. "Now, hold still. I have to fix your hair."

A knock sounded on the chapel door.

"Who goes there?" Katie boomed out.

The door opened, and Tracy timidly stepped inside with the bridal basket full of just what Katie and Christy needed to freshen up. Mom followed Tracy, and a moment later, Grandma joined them.

The door lurched open again, flooding the small chapel with light as Marti made her entrance. "The guests are beginning to arrive," she announced. "I've checked with the caterers. Everything is right on schedule. Looks as if the weather cooperated nicely. It's not too hot. Now, who needs a breath mint? Christy?"

Marti fussed with Christy's veil and her skirt for another ten minutes. The photographer came in to capture a few shots, and then Christy's dad joined them for his photos in the chapel with Christy. He looked uncomfortable in what he called his "monkey suit." But Christy thought he looked dashing and classy and so did her mom.

The photographer clicked off half a dozen shots. Christy turned to Katie and quietly asked if she could get Christy a drink of water.

"Right here," Marti said. "I had the caterers deliver a case of bottled water. It's here in the corner. Anyone else?"

They all grabbed a bottle, and for a moment the chapel was quiet. Christy looked at her mom and then at her dad. Marti looked at her watch. "Time for the mother of the bride, the grandmother of the bride, and me to exit. The ushers are out there for us. Can you think of anything else you need or want, Christina, dear?"

"No, I'm fine. I'm ready. Thank you for everything. All of you. Thanks."

"I'll see you at the end of the aisle." Mom cheerfully gave Christy a peck on the cheek.

"Check her for lipstick on that cheek," Marti instructed. "And, Katie, for goodness' sake, pull the veil over her face. Make sure it's straight all around. And Tracy? You listen for your cue now."

"I will," Tracy said.

Christy hung back as Katie adjusted her veil. She wrapped her grandmother's hankie around the stem handle of her bouquet. The handkerchief was already moist. If she actually needed to use it for tears, it might not do much to dry them. But it was helping her hands at the moment, and that was important.

A few silent minutes passed as Dad fidgeted with his collar. Katie opened the chapel's door a crack and watched to give Tracy her signal to march down the white runner. After Tracy, Katie would go. Then Christy and her dad would join the procession.

Glancing at her dad, Christy noticed he was tearing up. She only remembered seeing him like this a few times before. "Daddy, are you okay?"

"I will be." He offered her a lopsided grin. "It's not every day a man walks down the aisle with his only daughter. I guess you're not my little mouse anymore, are you?"

Christy felt a lump in her throat. He hadn't called her his little mouse in years. When she was growing up on their Wisconsin dairy farm, one of her favorite pastimes had been to follow her dad around in the barn. He was so big she could easily hide behind him. He would scoop her up in his arms, lift her over his head, and bellow for the cows to hear, "Look, I've found a little mouse! Listen to her squeak."

"I promise, Daddy," Christy said softly, "I'll always be your little mouse."

"And I'll always be as proud of you and thankful for you as I am at this very moment."

"That's my cue," Katie said over her shoulder as she exited. "Get ready now, you two."

Christy reached under her veil and dabbed the corner of each eye with her grandma's handkerchief. She linked her arm through her dad's and adjusted her bouquet.

"All right," Dad said, composing himself. "This is it."

Right on cue, Christy stepped out of the cool chapel
20into the brightness of the May afternoon. The guests shifted in their seats,
and she could feel their eyes on her,
watching her approach the end of the
white runner with her arm linked through her dad's.
She couldn't see Todd yet and guessed he couldn't see
her, either.

Christy and her father came to the end of the rows
of chairs. At her feet, a straight white runner led directly to the arch. She knew that under the decorated
arch stood her groom, dressed in a classy black tux
waiting for her, just as he had promised he would be
that enchanting morning in December right after she
had promised she would be his bride.

Christy drew in a deep breath. She lifted her eyes
under her veil and looked beyond the long white runner to the groom, her groom. And, oh, the look on his
face! This patient, relentless man waiting for her at the
end of the long aisle was so deeply in love with her

that he didn't even attempt to wipe the tears that were coursing down his cheeks.

As Christy watched Todd, he surprised her by lifting his arms and holding out his hands, inviting her to come to him. Those familiar hands that still bore the scars of his accident were welcoming her.

Christy put one foot in front of the other and kept walking.

Doug began to strum his guitar. That's when the next unexpected "random factor" occurred. Instead of Doug's singing a familiar wedding song as he had done at the rehearsal, Todd began to sing to Christy. His rich voice swirled around her, wooing her, beckoning her.

> "I have come into the garden, seeking you,
> There is no one else I desire, only you
> How beautiful you are, my love.
> Your eyes, watching from behind your veil
> As here I stand, calling for you to come
> Take me into your heart. Be with me
> Forever.
> How long have I waited for this moment,
> For this day. I will never leave you.
> My heart is ever toward you.
> Come into the garden, my beloved.
> Come, be my bride,
> Take my heart in yours,
> And I will be yours
> Forever."

Christy's last footstep brought her to the trellis just as Todd sang the word *forever*. Her heart pounded wildly. She recognized the tune. Todd had been humming it for months. This was the song he had been working on since the night they had become engaged; yet all these months she had only heard him hum or play the melody. She recognized the words were based on Scripture, from the Song of Solomon. When Todd had worked on the song, she had thought it was a worship song directed toward the Lord. And knowing Todd, ultimately it was.

But today, it was her song. She was his bride. He was her bridegroom. This was their forever moment. And Todd hadn't taken his eyes off her.

Pastor Ross spoke into the great chasm that separated Todd from Christy and said, "Who gives this woman to be united in holy matrimony with this man?"

Christy's father cleared his throat. All he was supposed to say was "Her mother and I." But Christy's dad apparently had a bit of the random factor at work in him, too. "Just as God, in love, gave Christina to us, now her mother and I, in love, give her to Todd."

Katie reached for Christy's bouquet, and with a squeeze, Dad placed Christy's hands into Todd's warm, strong, familiar hands. Todd ran his thumb across the gold Forever ID bracelet she had worn on her right wrist all these years.

"At last," Todd whispered.

That's when Christy started to cry. She had managed to keep the tears back all the way down the aisle. That was probably because so many surprises had kept her off guard and because Todd had been so fixed on her. But now she caught a quavering breath and felt a tear tip over the edge of her lower eyelid and trickle down her cheek. An entire flock of tears followed.

Todd's gaze remained fixed on Christy as hers was fixed on him. They barely blinked. They barely moved. The pastor spoke about the sacredness of this union. A song followed. Doug, this time. Christy barely heard. She was lost, swimming in the depths of her love for the man who stood beside her under this holy trellis and held her hands so tenderly.

The song ended, and Pastor Ross asked Christy to repeat her vows after him. Suddenly she was relieved she wasn't relying on her memory to repeat the long, elaborate vows she had written to Todd.

With a clear yet small voice, she repeated, "I, Christy, take you, Todd, to be my lawfully wedded husband. I promise to love, honor, and cherish you for better or for worse, for richer or for poorer, in sickness and in health, till death do us part."

Next came Todd's repeating of the vows. "I, Todd, take you, Christy, to be my lawfully wedded wife. I promise . . ." He squeezed her hands tighter. "To love, honor, and cherish you for better or for worse, for richer or for poorer, in sickness and in health, till death do us part."

"Now will you pray with me," Pastor Ross said.

Todd helped Christy to kneel down on the padded bench under the trellis. They bowed their heads as the pastor prayed for God's blessing on their marriage and on the children God may choose to bless them with.

"As you wish," Christy and Todd both whispered at the end of the prayer. Todd's strong grip held Christy by the elbow as they stood up.

"What token do you give as a symbol of your love for Christy?"

"A ring," Todd answered. His dad stepped forward and handed Christy's ring to Todd.

"Repeat after me," the pastor said. "As evidence of the promise we now make before God and these witnesses, with this ring, I thee wed."

Todd repeated the words and slid the wedding ring onto Christy's finger. In another surprise, he then lifted her ring finger to his lips and sealed his promise with a kiss.

"Christy," the pastor said, "what token do you give as a symbol of your love for Todd?"

"A ring," Christy said.

She turned only slightly and saw Katie's steady hand right there, holding out Todd's wedding band. Christy took the ring and repeated, "As evidence of the promise we now make before God and these witnesses, with this ring, I thee wed."

She slid the ring onto Todd's finger. Then she followed Todd's example and lifted his hand under her veil, where she sealed her promise with a kiss on his finger.

"In the name of the Father and of the Son and of the Holy Spirit, I now pronounce you man and wife. You may kiss the bride."

Christy stopped breathing. It seemed as if the whole world, including the dancing palm trees, had come to a sudden hush.

Slowly, tenderly, Todd took the ends of her delicate wedding veil and lifted it over her head. He looked on her as if he had never seen anything so wonderful, so beautiful, and so amazing in his life. Todd paused. He seemed to be drawing in the fragrance of the flowers that crowned her head. Moving closer, he slid both his hands along her jaw line until her hair was entwined in his fingers.

Christy tilted her face toward his and closed her eyes.

With all the tenderness of a patient man and all the passion of nearly six years of waiting, Todd kissed Christy. And she, with equal passion and patience, kissed him back.

As they lingered in their embrace, a gentle breeze came dancing toward them, snatching the fragrance from the flowers in Christy's hair and scattering sweetness across the meadow. The wind swirled through the palm trees. It almost sounded as if they were applauding.

In the holiness of that timeless moment, Todd whispered, "I love you, my Kilikina. Forever."

"And I love you," she whispered as silent tears raced down her cheeks. "Forever."

Then stepping from under their trellis, Christy heard a strong, steady voice behind her announcing the words that she knew would change her life forever. Until that moment, this one sentence had only echoed in the corner of her heart where she stored her most precious dreams.

Today, the words were real. All the stars of heaven were in her eyes as she gazed at the man who now stood beside her and the pastor said,

"It is my privilege to introduce to you for the very first time, Mr. and Mrs. Todd Spencer."

The Series That
STARTED IT ALL

Janette Oke is known and loved for her gentle tales of love emerging in the hearts of men and women struggling to lead lives of faith on the open prairie. Beginning with the story of Marty and Clark Davis' marriage in *Love Comes Softly*, Janette unwinds a romance as deep and resonant as any that have been written.

For decades readers have flocked to these books for a reassuring tale of how God can bring greater meaning to the love shared by two people—during times of joy and times of suffering. Now you can join those millions of fans and enjoy these quiet and spiritually enriching tales.

Love Comes Softly ❖ Love's Enduring Promise
Love's Long Journey ❖ Love's Abiding Joy
Love's Unending Legacy ❖ Love's Unfolding Dream
Love Takes Wing ❖ Love Finds a Home